LESS-THAN-INNOCENT *Invitation*

SHIRLEY ROGERS

Silhouette® Desire

Published by Silhouette Books

America's Publisher of Contemporary Romance

Special thanks and acknowledgment are given to Shirley Rogers for her contribution to the TEXAS CATTLEMAN'S CLUB: THE SECRET DIARY series.

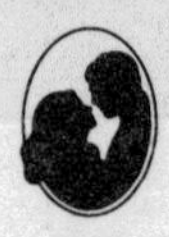

SILHOUETTE BOOKS

ISBN 0-373-76671-8

LESS-THAN-INNOCENT INVITATION

This edition published by arrangement with Harlequin Books S.A.

Visit Silhouette Books at www.eHarlequin.com

Printed in U.S.A.

Books by Shirley Rogers

Silhouette Desire

Cowboys, Babies and Shotgun Vows #1176
Conveniently His #1266
A Cowboy, a Bride & a Wedding Vow #1344
Baby of Fortune #1384
One Wedding Night... #1434
Her Texan Temptation #1481
Terms of Surrender #1615
Business Affairs #1632
Less-than-Innocent Invitation #1671

SHIRLEY ROGERS

lives in Virginia with her husband, two cats and an adorable Maltese named Blanca. She has two grown children, a son and a daughter. As a child, she was known for having a vivid imagination. It wasn't until she started reading romances that she realized her true destiny was writing them! Besides reading, she enjoys traveling, seeing movies and spending time with her family.

Prologue

From the diary of Jessamine Golden
August 10, 1910

Dear Diary,
Something happened today that I will always cherish in my heart. Something wonderful. Sheriff Brad Webster kissed me.

Me. A woman who walks on the opposite side of everything he stands for.

Though we have chosen different directions in life—his honorable and noble, mine a path that creates a barrier between us—this magnificent, proud man kissed me.

It was a glorious ending to a perfect day. Brad took me on a picnic down by the lake, and we spent a whole afternoon together on a blanket in the shade of a willow tree. As we talked, he took my hand in his, and I grew warm all over.

As the sun set low in the sky and our day together began to slip away, Brad leaned close to me and stroked my lips with his thumb. Every single inch of my body responded to his touch. My skin tingled and my face flushed hot, so hot that I knew he could tell how much he affected me. He smiled at me then and, for a moment, I thought he was going to laugh at me.

But, he kissed me instead. Oh, my, he kissed me. And his kiss was so tender, yet full of promise. His arms held me with gentle strength, and I wanted it to never end. In that instant, I forgot that our lives are worlds apart. I forgot everything except being with Brad.

Oh, diary, it felt as if the entire universe had shifted, and for that moment in time, that one captivating moment, I wanted only to be with him for the rest of my life.

But that can never be, can it?

I wish with all my heart that our circumstances were different, that the path I must follow wasn't against the code of honor Brad holds. But just as the darkness of night has fallen, the time to change my course in life has passed. Tonight I will fall asleep and dream of another time when Brad and I could be together. A time that embraces forever.

One

Logan Voss checked his watch for the third time in the space of fifteen minutes. Damn! The 125th Anniversary celebration of Royal, Texas, had started only an hour ago, but he felt as if he'd been there for hours. From the excitement in the air, it appeared to be a huge success.

Scanning the festively decorated ballroom of the Texas Cattleman's Club, he took a sip of the whiskey he'd been nursing for the past half hour. The August event was in full swing. Conversation and laughter flowed just beneath the song being belted out by a local country band. Logan knew just about everyone here. Many of the men were members of their elite club, some of them the same men who had talked him into attending this party.

He spotted Jake Thorne and Christine Travers dancing and smiled. Seeing as Jake had sworn he wasn't ready for anything serious with a woman, and most especially with Christine, Logan couldn't have helped but give his friend a hard time when he'd greeted him earlier in the evening. Now Jake had taken the proverbial fall, and he and Christine were planning to be married

Better him than me, Logan thought, loosening the tie around his neck. He'd been down that road before, had ended up buying his freedom from a marriage that never should have taken place.

Despite their divorce and financial settlement, Logan held no hard feelings for his ex-wife. It had been mostly his fault that their relationship hadn't worked out. Though he'd failed to realize it at the time, he'd married her for all the wrong reasons—his breakup with Melissa Mason being at the top of the list.

Melissa.

Hell, he hadn't thought about Melissa in what…at least a month. That was probably a record for him. Even after more than ten years apart, she usually crossed his mind every week or so. It was said that you never really forget your first love. Logan had to agree. Melissa's beautiful smile and sexy green eyes still haunted him.

He sighed and shoved away from the wall. What was wrong with him? The last person he needed to think about tonight was Melissa.

"Hey, Logan. What are you doing over here by yourself?"

"Mark." Logan greeted Mark Hartman, another single member of their elite club. After the death of his brother and sister-in-law, Mark had been named the guardian of his nine-month-old niece. How he managed taking care of a baby, operating his ranch and running a self-defense studio puzzled Logan, especially since Mark seemed to have trouble holding onto a nanny. "Actually, I was just thinking about leaving," Logan admitted.

"You're kidding, right?" Mark took a sip from his glass, then gestured with the same hand toward the crowd. "With all these pretty ladies to dance with?"

"I notice you're not out there." From their conversations, Logan had learned Mark was also hesitant about becoming involved with a woman. Years ago while he was overseas on a mission, the ex-marine's wife had been abducted and killed. Though he rarely spoke of her death, from the sadness that lingered in his friend's eyes, Logan suspected Mark had never gotten over it.

"Point taken." Mark drained the last of his drink. "Some celebration, though. There's even a reporter with a crew here from a Houston television station."

"Yeah?" Logan wasn't really interested in the coverage of the city's anniversary. Working his ranch didn't leave much time to watch television. Even if he met the reporter, he doubted he'd recognize the guy.

Mark nodded his head, indicating a group of people across the room. "A woman. Pretty, too. I heard she used to live here."

The small hairs on Logan's neck prickled. He shifted his attention to the crowd. He didn't see anyone who he suspected could be the reporter. But… He scanned the group again, slower this time, and his gaze landed on a woman, her back turned to him.

Layers of auburn curls cascaded past her shoulders. She wore a sparkly white cocktail dress made to enhance her slender figure. As if she sensed him watching her, she looked in his direction.

Logan's breath whooshed out as if he'd received a hard punch to his midsection.

Melissa.

"Damn," he muttered.

"You know her?" Mark asked, not missing the change in Logan's demeanor.

"I used to." Logan tracked her movements as she lifted her hand and brushed a strand of hair from her eyes. Every muscle in his body tightened.

How could she have an effect on him after all this time? It had been more than ten years since he'd set eyes on her. But watching her now, it felt as if it had only been yesterday when he'd fallen in love with her and asked her to marry him.

Pain sliced through him. Logan remembered only too well how she'd come to his ranch the day after she'd accepted his proposal and told him she'd changed her mind and was leaving town. Melissa had spoken of leaving Royal when they'd begun dating. But after seeing each other nearly every day, he'd believed her when she'd said she loved him. Apparently she hadn't meant it.

The music throbbed around him as he thought about the last month he'd spent with her. Everything in his life had fallen into place. He'd always loved the Wild Spur, the ranch he'd been raised on. He'd loved it as much as his younger brother, Bart, who had been spoiled by their father, hated it. He'd moved into Royal as soon as he graduated and Logan rarely ran into him.

When their father had died of a heart attack, the

brothers had made plans for Logan to buy out Bart's portion. The plan suited both of them. They'd never been close and Bart had wanted no part of the Wild Spur. But neither of them had known about the stipulation their father had put in his will.

The first son to marry would get the Wild Spur.

At first angry at their father, Logan and Bart had discussed how to get around the will. Then they realized they didn't have to worry. Logan was already in love with Melissa. When they married, everything would be his and he still could buy out Bart's part of the inheritance.

So he'd proposed to Melissa and she'd accepted.

Except a day later she'd changed her mind.

Without looking back, she'd dismissed him from her life. He hadn't been able to tell her she was ripping him apart inside.

Vulnerability wasn't an emotion Logan was familiar with. Losing his mother at the age of eleven, he'd been raised by a demanding father who hadn't encouraged sharing feelings. Logan had learned to hold what he thought and wanted to express inside.

He watched now as Melissa laughed at something the man beside her said and his chest began to ache. Afraid that she'd met someone else, he hadn't gone after Melissa, hadn't given her a chance to hurt him further. He'd always believed himself a smart man. He knew he should let bygones be bygones. The last thing he needed to do was to stir up unwanted memories. But damn it, he wanted answers. He wanted to know why she'd left, why she hadn't talked to him.

Would he accomplish that if he confronted her?

Would he see a fraction of the pain that he'd felt for years in Melissa's face? Would that make him feel any better? Would it heal his heart and let him move past the torment he'd endured?

And how would he react if it didn't? What if she looked at him as though she barely remembered him? God, if she did, he didn't know how he'd handle it. Could he walk away from her and salvage his dignity?

What if she gazed at him and he saw regret in her lovely green eyes? It wasn't as if they could pick up where they left off before, right?

And he wouldn't want to, anyway. He wouldn't trust his heart to her again. No, sir. Not again. But he damn sure wanted some answers from her. And if she didn't want to talk, he'd figure out some way to convince her.

He threw back the remainder of his drink, then set the glass down with a thud on a nearby table. Whether hearing the truth from Melissa would heal his pain or not, he deserved to know what had happened and he wasn't letting her leave town until he knew.

"See you later," he muttered to Mark. Logan's boots echoed with a steady beat on the hardwood floor as he started across the room.

With something close to fear squeezing her chest, Melissa watched Logan Voss storm across the ballroom, aimed in her direction. No, not fear, she quickly corrected herself. Anxiety? Oh, yeah. Anticipation? Most definitely. Awareness? Yes, even awareness, she admitted to herself, unable to deny the quick stir of her heart.

From the moment she'd been given the assignment

to cover the anniversary celebration of her hometown of Royal, Texas, she'd known the odds were high that she'd run into Logan.

But considering the promotion she'd been promised if she did the story, the risk had been worth it. Of course, that was *before* she'd arrived.

And before she'd seen Logan.

She should have known that she'd run into him tonight. All day while filming in Royal, she'd been feeling edgy, almost sensing impending doom about to strike her. Now that doom was heading straight for her in the form of one very determined and grim-faced rancher.

Melissa quickly searched the room for the nearest exit. After the rumors she'd heard about the secret missions of the wealthy members of the Texas Cattleman's Club, she'd wanted to satisfy her curiosity by talking with a few of the members.

Too bad she had to cut her visit short.

Hoping to escape before Logan reached her, she broke off her conversation with her videographer and sound person, Rick Johnson. However, before she could take a step, Logan blocked her path. Her gaze traveled up his broad chest, over his set jaw and finally connected with his gorgeous gray-green eyes.

She acknowledged what any warm-blooded female had to admit—the years had been awfully good to Logan. He was what, thirty-four now, three years older than herself. The only wrinkles she could make out on his sexy face were tiny lines crinkled around his eyes. Laugh lines, weren't they called?

Only Logan didn't look as though he had laughing on his mind.

Steeling herself, Melissa offered Logan a polite smile, one she'd perfected as a reporter. She'd be damned if she'd let him know just how hard her heart was beating.

"Logan, hi. It's been a long time." It was an effort to keep her voice light and appear at ease when it took all of her strength just to stand there in front of him.

"Over ten years," Logan replied, then cursed under his breath for making it sound as if he'd been counting. At least she knew who he was. One hurdle crossed.

Melissa tilted her head as if trying to recall the time, when in reality it was etched permanently in her mind. "Yes, I guess you're right. How have you been?" she asked, her tone more nostalgic than she'd intended. It wasn't every day she made polite conversation with the only man she'd ever loved, the same man who had ruthlessly used her for his own greed.

Logan propped his hand on his hip as his gaze dropped lazily over her. "Well, sweetheart, I've been just dandy. How about you?"

Melissa's breath dammed in her lungs. Though barely discernable, she caught the underlying sarcasm in his voice. What did *he* have to feel put off about? He was the one who had hurt *her* all those years ago.

But she refused to be baited by him. Dredging up unpleasant memories was not on her list of things to do while in town. "I've been fine. I'm in Royal covering the anniversary celebration," she explained, feeling it was safer to keep their conversation on a neutral subject.

He remained silent, forcing Melissa to pick up the

conversation again. "I'm a reporter for WKHU, a television station in Houston."

Logan's jaw tautened. "So you got what you wanted." *A life away from Royal.*

Away from me.

He mentally shut himself off from the hurt of their breakup. Crossing his arms, he stared at her. He'd heard rumors that Melissa was a journalist somewhere, but the rare times her name came up in a conversation, he excused himself because he didn't want to know where she was.

Or who she was with.

Houston. All these years she'd been here in the state of Texas. Hell, what did it matter? She'd made her choice a long time ago.

Melissa stiffened her carriage. "A life as a reporter? Yes." Her answer held little truth. She'd wanted him. Forever. Until she'd learned the selfish truth of why he'd asked her to marry him.

Logan raised a skeptical eyebrow. She frowned, a bit put off by his cynicism. "Don't look so shocked. I've been doing this a long time, and I've worked hard, taking assignments other reporters have turned down."

Including coming back to this town.

After years of proving herself by covering every type of story imaginable, she'd begun to believe if she was ever going to get a desk assignment, she might have to move to another station in a larger market. Although she liked and respected the station's news director, Jason Bellamy, he had yet to give her a chance.

Until last week. She had Jason's word that if she covered this one last story, she'd be promoted to a weekend news position becoming available in a month. Her dreams lay before her. She only had to complete this last assignment.

"Actually, I'm impressed," Logan admitted. And he was. His love hadn't been enough to make Melissa happy, but apparently she'd found what she'd been searching for in her work. Had her satisfaction also come in the form of another man? He glanced at her left hand and noticed it was free of any wedding rings.

"Thank you." From the hard edge in his voice, Melissa doubted his sincerity. Their parting had been traumatic for her. How had he handled it? She wanted to know, but she wasn't going to ask.

Silence fell between them. With her emotions in turmoil, she had to get out of there. She sent Rick a desperate look, but he was engaged in a conversation with Daniel, her story producer, who had come to Royal as part of their crew.

The upbeat country tune changed to a slow, heady song about lost love. The melancholy words of the tune mimicked her past relationship with Logan. One of her favorites, she'd often played it when she'd wondered if she'd done the right thing breaking up with him.

"Dance?"

Logan's request jerked her from her thoughts. "What?"

"Would you like to dance?" He wasn't about to let her get away. Taking a step toward her, he closed the distance between them, her panicked look giving him a sense of satisfaction. Apparently she wasn't as immune to him as she wanted him to believe.

"With you?" Surprised he'd asked, she struggled to maintain her composure, knowing she stood little chance of holding herself together if he touched her.

He gave her a wry grin, the idea of holding her in his arms more appealing than he wanted to admit. "Well, sweetheart, since I'm the one who's asking..."

"I, um, I'm not sure that's such a good idea." Melissa shivered at the thought of being held again by Logan. Until now, she'd compartmentalized her feelings for him. Dancing with him would be tantamount to opening the lid on her personal Pandora's box.

Trying to stall, she glanced around, only to notice that several of her crew were watching them with more than a passing interest. So were some of Royal's finest citizens, people she'd known when she'd lived there. She quietly groaned. The last thing she wanted to do was to cause a scene right there in the middle of the ballroom.

"It's just a dance, Melissa," Logan coolly stated. At the indecision in her eyes a sudden rush of desperation shot through him. He *wanted* her to say yes—but for all the wrong reasons.

Yeah, sure, he wanted answers from her, but he found himself wanting to hold her once again. The knot in his stomach twisted a little tighter. At sixteen she'd been cute, at twenty, pretty. Now, at thirty-one, she was flat-out beautiful. Her long chestnut hair fell in curls around her face, setting off her fascinating green eyes. His gaze drifted lower, over her bare shoulders and slim, athletic figure. Her dress hid very little of her perfect skin. No wonder the television industry had her in front of the camera.

Shaking his head, Logan forced himself to stop thinking about how beautiful she was and centered his attention on what he really wanted from her. Answers about why she'd left. If she'd lied about loving him. And now, after seeing her again, he needed to prove to himself that these new feelings of awareness were based on nostalgia and nothing more, that the desire he'd felt for her all those years ago was long gone.

"Are you here with someone?" Melissa asked. She looked at his hand, searching for a wedding ring but finding none. She told herself it didn't mean anything. Because work on a ranch could sometimes be dangerous, even if he *was* married, he probably didn't wear a ring.

He grinned at her. "No."

"All right," Melissa answered, more than a little surprised at his response. And curious. Did that mean there was no one special in his life? Or that he was alone just for this evening?

She held out her hand and Logan closed his around it. They walked to the dance floor, and a shiver of anticipation whispered through her as he pulled her into his arms. Her lungs constricted with a needy ache. She was a fool to do this, to be this close to him, to let him anywhere near her heart. Even as she acknowledged she was playing with fire, her hand traitorously trailed across his shoulder to rest close to his neck.

Closing her eyes she breathed in his scent, and the enticing, woodsy smell took her back to another time, another place, when he'd held her in his arms in more intimate ways as his big hands caressed her skin until she'd trembled with anticipation.

Oh, this is not a good idea, her mind chanted over and over again. She leaned away, placing some much-needed distance between them. Opening her eyes, she searched his face to see if she'd had any effect on him. His emotionless mask, however, gave her no clue to his thoughts. She quickly looked away. "It's a nice party," she commented, struggling to ground herself.

Logan nodded. "The town's planned a lot of events to commemorate its anniversary."

She gave him a practiced, on-camera smile. "And the Texas Cattleman's Club is doing its part."

"We aim to please."

Which meant he was now a member of the Texas Cattleman's Club. She found that interesting, but under the circumstances, she wasn't about to stroke his ego by pursuing that topic. "A lot of work has gone into putting this ball together."

"It isn't every day the town has something this exciting to celebrate." Logan felt the softness of Melissa's hand in his and was suddenly very glad that he hadn't left the ball. Not that he intended to have more than a dance with her.

His mind drifted to the last time he'd made love to her, how she'd… No he wasn't going to punish himself with the memories. What they had shared together was a long time ago.

Done.

Over.

He'd asked her to dance to confront her, not to reminisce about how it felt to hold her, to touch her skin, to run his hands over her body.

His goal was to get her to tell him why she'd broken up with him.

Nothing more.

Maybe once he knew the truth he could truly forget her.

God knows he'd tried.

"When my story producer heard about the legend surrounding Jessamine Golden, he insisted on coming with me and my videographer to learn about it firsthand."

"Yeah, history has it she was quite an outlaw," he answered. "A lot of people believe the gold she stole is still hidden around here somewhere." His struggle to keep Melissa at a distance was proving more difficult than he'd imagined. Her perfume filled his senses. Her scent hadn't changed. He'd never quite forgotten her smell—like sunshine and lavender.

Excitement lit her eyes. "If it's true and the gold was found, it would be quite a story." Tempted to stay in Royal and dig up some additional material on Jessamine Golden and the treasure she'd supposedly stolen and hidden, Melissa hesitated. If she did, she'd chance running into Logan again—a risk she wasn't ready to take. This one encounter with him was definitely enough.

Truthfully, her heart had never quite healed. She'd thought she'd successfully dealt with her feelings for Logan, but now in his arms, she realized she hadn't. Though not in love with him anymore, her emotions for him still went deep. It was best to finish this dance and say goodbye.

"So, is this what you've doing all these years?" Logan asked, changing the subject to one that would help him keep his focus. "Chasing leads and reporting the news?"

"Pretty much." She lifted a shoulder in a soft shrug as they slowly moved to the music, conscious of how Logan used that moment to pull her closer. Rather than make an issue of feeling his hard, lean body pressed to hers, she pretended that she didn't notice. Or notice how easy it would be to lean the few inches separating them and kiss him. She focused on his chin instead of looking into his eyes. "Of course, I haven't always been given assignments like attending glamorous events. I've covered a lot of stories over the years, paid my dues, as they say."

"Was it worth it?" Logan asked, his voice low, yet determined. He'd planned on waiting until the right moment to ask her, but the words spilled out of his mouth. He told himself it had nothing to do with the way she felt.

Melissa's eyes grew wary. "I enjoy what I do."

"That's not what I asked." A hard edge crept into his voice, an underlying current of tension he hadn't been able to conceal.

"I thought you wanted to dance for old time's sake." Melissa stopped moving and tried to disengage from him. She came up short when he wouldn't let her go.

"I did," he told her, aware he wasn't being totally truthful. Grimacing, he admitted, "But I also want to know what made you break our engagement. You owe me that."

"No, Logan, I don't." When she pulled away this time, he let her go. It startled her as much as when he hadn't.

"The hell you don't."

"This is ridiculous! Why would you want to dredge up old memories anyway, Logan? What happened between us was a lifetime ago. It's water under the bridge. Over." Her lungs lacked air. Calming herself, she managed to take in a short breath.

His jaw hardened. "I guess maybe to you it is."

Melissa eyes widened. Did his comment mean that to him it wasn't? His rigid stance revealed nothing more than that she'd provoked his anger. Well, she was pretty angry now herself. How dare he imply that their breakup was her fault? "I'm not responsible for what happened between us, Logan Voss. You are and you know it."

Logan stared at her in disbelief. "Me?"

"Yes, you!"

"You're the one who left, Melissa." His tone was sharp as he tried to speak over the music. He glanced around the room, irritated as people started to turn toward them. Damn, this was getting out of hand, and he wasn't about to give anyone a show. Frustrated, he grabbed her wrist.

"What are you doing?"

"I don't know about you, but I'm not too crazy about providing tonight's entertainment. Let's take this outside."

Two

"Let me go!" Melissa's voice rose a notch. At that moment, the music ended and she realized he had a point. Many of the guests had stopped dancing and were watching them with something between amusement, surprise and blatant curiosity. Heat burned her face. Back in Royal only one day and already Logan was turning her life upside down

Logan dropped her hand. "We can go out the quiet way or not. The decision's yours."

Forcing herself to smile, she nodded. "Fine." He started walking toward the door. She kept up with his long strides, her heels clicking on the polished hardwood floor.

As soon as they entered the impressive foyer, Logan came to an abrupt halt beneath the glow of a rustic antler chandelier. Preventing herself from running into him, Melissa steadied herself with her palm on his sculptured back.

She sucked in a breath. As his muscles shifted beneath her hand, memories of making love with him dulled her senses. Giving her head a shake, she stepped back.

"Are you crazy?" she demanded, glaring at him. "People were beginning to stare at us back there."

Logan glanced toward the door, then back at her. "They wouldn't have even noticed us if you'd just answered my question."

Melissa tossed her head back. "I have no intention of getting into a discussion about…about…" She stopped speaking and took a calming breath. Why hadn't she heeded her inner warnings about returning to her hometown and the possibility of seeing Logan again? If her promotion hadn't been riding on this assignment, she would never have come back. Never have taken the risk of seeing him.

Ever.

"Look, this is ridiculous."

"Is it?" He leaned toward her. "Ridiculous is the way you suddenly left, Melissa." His hands went to his hips. "More than once I've tried to figure out why. What went wrong between us?" Cursing under his breath, he held her gaze. He didn't admit that thinking about what had happened that last day, thinking about her and what they'd shared, could still drive him crazy.

"I didn't just take off," she reminded him, her tone scorching. "I came to see you."

He made a sound of disgust. "Yeah, to toss my ring

in my face and tell me you were leaving. Why?" he demanded. "Was it because you fell in love with someone else?" Though he braced himself for her answer, he didn't want to believe she'd been seeing another man. It would kill him.

"No!" Her face drained of color. "Is that what you thought?"

"Hell, I didn't know what to think. I believed you loved me. Then all of a sudden, you were telling me you didn't want to be married." His voice softened. "Do you even remember what we had together?"

Melissa licked her lips. "Of course I do." As soon as she said the words, she wished them back.

Logan closed the distance between them. Unable to stop himself from touching her, he cupped his hand around her neck. Despite the anger that had simmered inside of him for so long, he wanted to pull her against him. "Do you, Melissa?" Something drove him to find out if she'd thought about him since she'd been gone, if she'd ever regretted leaving.

Swallowing hard, Melissa's eyes locked with his. Oh, how she'd loved this man. "Yes," she whispered.

Logan lowered his head, his lips lingering just above hers. "Then you remember just how good we were together."

Her gaze drifted lower to his mouth. "Oh, Logan."

At that moment the door to the ballroom whisked open. Logan straightened and stepped away from her as a man entered the foyer and walked hurriedly toward them.

What the hell was he doing? He had no business even thinking about kissing Melissa Mason. He'd let his heart get tangled up with her before and their relationship had ended badly. Hadn't he learned his lesson?

Apparently not. After only a few minutes in her company, his mind had drifted to the memories of touching her.

Kissing her.

He wanted to know if she tasted as sweet as he remembered.

No, it was more than curiosity. Dancing with her had stirred up all kinds of emotions inside him, made him aware of her in ways that time had blurred.

"Melissa, there you are!"

"Daniel!" Expelling a breath, Melissa turned away from Logan as her producer approached, relieved he'd chosen that moment to find her.

After all the years apart from Logan, she never would have dreamed she'd give in so easily to him again, but God knows, if left alone a minute longer, she would have kissed him. Now that she knew she wasn't immune to him, she'd keep her distance until she could get out of town.

She gestured toward him. "This is an old friend of mine, Logan Voss. Logan, Daniel Graves. He's the story producer for the feature on Royal's anniversary."

"Mr. Voss."

Logan held out his hand. "Call me Logan," he told the man as he tried to absorb Melissa's description of him as an "old friend." It stung more than it should have.

Daniel clasped his hand with a firm grip. "It's a pleasure to meet you."

"I hope you're enjoying yourself at the ball," Logan said as he studied the man. Twice his own age, Daniel

Graves was thin and wiry with a nervous energy that made him look as if he was fidgeting even while he stood still.

"I am." He turned toward Melissa, his eyes wide with excitement. "And I've just heard the most exciting news. I was talking to one of the guests and heard that some of Jessamine Golden's personal belongings have turned up at an auction!"

"Yes, I know. I heard about it when I arrived in town yesterday and I have notes on it," Melissa told him. "Apparently they auctioned off a saddle bag and a few other things. I was going to discuss the information with you on our trip back to Houston."

"So you already know about the map?" Daniel asked.

Melissa frowned. "I know there was a map of some kind, but I fail to see what you're so excited about."

"Inside the saddlebag was a treasure map."

She rolled her eyes. "Daniel, please don't tell me you're falling for that tale," she scoffed.

The producer ignored her remark and turned to Logan. "You don't seem to be surprised."

Shaking his head, he replied, "The legend of Jessamine Golden burying a cache of gold bars somewhere around here has been circulating for years. The map and the rest of her items are on display at the Historical Society Museum." The common thought among his friends at the Cattleman's Club was that if Jessamine had indeed heisted the gold, the map was proof she'd intended to come back for it. Something must have prevented her from returning.

"I hope to see them while I'm here," Daniel stated.

Logan settled back into a comfortable stance. "One of my friends, Jake Thorne, donated them to the museum after he bought them at the auction."

"The same Jake Thorne who's running for mayor?" Melissa asked.

"Yeah. Jake outbid Christine, who is now his fiancée."

"Really?" She frowned. "Why would he do that? Was he trying to increase the amount of money for charity or something?"

Logan shrugged. "I don't know. They weren't dating at the time. Christine wanted the items for the museum. Jake eventually made it up to her by donating them."

At the excitement building in Daniel's eyes, Logan remarked, "You know, it's only speculation that the map may lead to a treasure."

"That's true. And we all know how rumors are always built out of proportion," Melissa said. She didn't want her producer getting ideas about staying in Royal any longer than they originally had planned. But from his excited expression he already seemed intrigued, which meant nothing but trouble for her. She was ready to leave Royal tonight, to put Logan and memories of their love affair behind her. Now, thanks to a hokey map, her plans were in jeopardy.

Daniel's excited expression faltered a fraction. "There's a chance that the map is real."

"Daniel—"

"You don't *know* it isn't and you won't if you don't look into the story. Also, one of the guests said he'd heard someone had vandalized an exhibit at the museum and it was close to where Jessamine's things are on display."

Melissa frowned. "Which exhibit?"

"The one on Edgar Halifax." Daniel looked at Logan. "Who was he?"

"Edgar was Royal's first mayor and is credited with establishing the town," Logan informed him. "He was shot and killed and the person responsible was never caught. For the anniversary celebration and because Gretchen Halifax, his descendant and also a mayoral candidate, pushed for it, an exhibit in his honor is on display at the museum."

"Do they have any idea why it was vandalized?" Melissa asked.

"Not from what I've heard." Daniel shifted his attention to his reporter.

She raised an eyebrow. "Sounds like someone has an ax to grind, but I fail to see any connection to Jessamine Golden's legend."

"That's where you come in," her producer told her. "We're going to stay in town for a few days. You can spend some time working on the connection, if there is one. It'll make a great addition to your story."

Melissa all but groaned, even though she had to admit that something suspicious was going on. Still, in her opinion it didn't warrant them staying in Royal. "I think we have enough footage and information for the story we're planning."

"Maybe for what we originally planned, but I've already talked to Jason. We're covering Royal's anniversary celebration, but we're also planning a series on historical mysteries. Let's investigate Jessamine Golden more thoroughly. And I want you to report on the vandalism when you put the story together. Do some digging. There's no telling what you could turn up."

"Jason?" Logan asked, noticing the panicked look on Melissa's face.

Melissa explained, "Jason Bellamy is the news director at our station." She turned toward her producer, her eyes wide. "This could take a while. Daniel, I don't think—"

"People love a mystery, and this one is rich with historic significance. You might even find a way to connect it to the town's celebration."

Logan watched the two of them with interest. By Melissa's replies and body language, it was clear she wasn't crazy about staying in town. Why? Because of him? He discounted that theory. She'd walked away from him before without batting an eye.

Well, he wanted her to stay until he found out what he wanted to know from her.

"Do you have hotel reservations?" he asked, hoping they didn't. If they hadn't made reservations, they were going to need a place to stay.

Melissa gave him a frustrated look. "No, we don't. We checked out today because we *weren't staying,*" she reminded her producer, pinning him with a hard stare. Remaining in Royal wasn't an option. Nearly kissing Logan tonight was enough to tell her that her feelings for him went deeper than their years apart could erase.

"Then you have a problem," Logan stated, already thinking about setting them up at his ranch. "You won't be able to get a hotel room."

"Nowhere in town?" her story producer asked. "Are you sure?"

Relief rushed through Melissa and she released a pent-up breath. "Well, that's that, then." She almost did a happy dance. Now they could leave. And if Daniel wanted a more in-depth piece on Royal, he could come back—with another reporter.

"Yes. Everything has been booked for weeks because of the celebration." Logan checked the time. "At this hour, you'd have to drive for miles before you'd find an available room, if you're lucky." As Daniel's face fell, Logan put his plan into action. "Tell you what. I'll be glad to help you out."

Daniel leaned toward Logan. "How?"

"I own a ranch just outside of town. I can put you and your crew up while you're here."

"What?" Melissa squeaked.

"That would be great." Daniel missed his reporter's look of alarm. "Thank you!"

"Wait a minute—"

"My pleasure." Ignoring Melissa's protest, Logan shook Daniel's hand, sealing the deal. "How many are in your crew?"

"Three. The two of us and Rick Johnson, our videographer and sound person."

"I have plenty of room. I'll give my housekeeper a call and let her know to expect you later tonight."

"Logan, wait!" Melissa grabbed his arm as he started to turn away. "We can't possibly impose on you."

He smiled at her. "It's the least I can do."

Not fooled by his innocent expression, she dropped

her hand. "So you're doing this for the town, is that it?" She knew better than to trust him. He had an ulterior motive, but at the moment she was at a loss as to what it could be.

Logan looked down at his arm where she'd touched him. He could swear he'd felt the heat of her through the fabric of his suit. His gaze swung up to her face. "What other reason could I have?"

"I don't know. Why don't you tell me?"

"None, I assure you, sweetheart. Now if you'll excuse me, I have a call to make."

She glanced at the bracelet watch on her arm. "It's late," she blurted, stopping him again, this time with only her words. "You can't expect your housekeeper to make up rooms for us at this hour."

Logan grinned at them both. "Wait until you meet Norah. Believe me, she won't mind a bit. She'll make you feel right at home."

Melissa's heart sank. *This can't be happening!* She did not want to stay in Royal.

And she surely did not want to stay at Logan's ranch.

That would be just too darn close to the man for comfort. The farther away from Logan she was, the better. She started to protest again, but Logan turned away and began dialing his cell phone.

Melissa frowned at Daniel. Though she wanted to argue about his decision to stay at Logan's ranch, how could she? Daniel would want to know her reasons. As it stood, her colleagues knew nothing about her past with Logan.

And she wanted to keep it that way.

"Staying on a ranch. This will be exciting," Daniel said, breaking into her thoughts.

"Yeah, exciting." Her voice revealed she was anything but. It was just her luck to have a boss who was a history buff.

Logan punched a button on his phone, then tucked it inside his jacket. He turned toward them. "Everything is all set. Norah will have your rooms ready for you by the time you arrive."

Daniel clapped him on the back. "We can't thank you enough, Logan."

Logan was glad things had turned in his favor. "The pleasure's mine." He looked at Melissa. "All mine, I assure you."

Daniel's face lit up like a Boy Scout earning his first merit badge. "If you'll give us directions to your ranch, we'll leave the celebration in a short while. The last thing we want is to be an inconvenience."

"That's not necessary. Stay as late as you like. I wouldn't want you to miss a minute of it." He gave Melissa a long look. Putting her on the defensive, he said, "Besides, Melissa can find the Wild Spur. She already knows the way, don't you sweetheart? I'll meet you when you arrive." Touching the brim of his hat, he walked away.

Her mouth dropping open, Melissa stared after him as he exited through the doublewide front doors. From her producer's silence, she knew Logan's comment had left him speechless, too. Facing him, she explained, "I knew Logan in high school." She hoped that would be enough information to satisfy his curiosity.

It didn't work. Daniel's raised eyebrows caused her stomach to wrench.

"I got the feeling there was more between the two of you than being school chums," he commented. "So there's another side to my wonderful workaholic reporter?"

Melissa's lips tightened into a straight line. "I am not a workaholic."

"No? Dear, you haven't been on a date in months."

"I've been busy working for a promotion, which Jason has promised me after this assignment," she reminded him.

"I know, and you'll get it. But that doesn't mean that you can't slow down occasionally, have a little fun."

"I do things for enjoyment. I went out with the gang last week."

Daniel shook his head. "Going out for drinks with a group of friends from work isn't the same as dating and you know it. You only travel in a pack." As if jolted by his own words, he looked at the door Logan had just left through, then back at Melissa.

"Don't go reading anything into that wicked mind of yours. I knew Logan a long time ago. That's all."

"Oh, really?" Daniel raised his dark, bushy eyebrows. "C'mon, Melissa. I'm surprised I'm not singed from the vibes between the two of you."

"What you were feeling is your imagination getting away from you."

"You can deny it all you want, but there's something going on between you and Logan Voss."

"Daniel, you're crazy! I haven't seen the man in years. How could there be anything between us?" Logically, it made sense and she hoped Daniel bought it. Because before he'd walked into the foyer and interrupted them, Logan had been about to kiss her. And she would have let him.

Worse, she would have kissed him back.

Oh, Lord, what had she been thinking? When she'd learned the reason Logan had wanted to marry her, her heart had broken in two. She'd prayed that Logan would come after her and tell her she'd been wrong to believe what she'd heard. But he hadn't. It had been years before she'd been able to think of dating again.

Now, back in Royal for a few hours, she'd been tempted by that same destructive path.

Exasperated, Melissa glared at Daniel. "Let's go into the party. There are a few more people I want to talk to."

"All right." Daniel followed her. "I'll find you, say, in about an hour." He opened the door for her. After she entered, he walked in behind her. "Let me know if you're ready to leave earlier."

Melissa nodded as she made her escape, Daniel's words echoing through her mind.

Let me know if you're ready to leave earlier.

Ha! As if that was even a possibility. The last place on earth she'd thought she'd end up tonight was at Logan's ranch.

There had to be some way to get out of going there. Perhaps Logan had been wrong. It was possible that the hotels weren't solidly booked. How could he even know that for sure, anyway?

She looked around for Rick. Since she'd ridden to Royal with him, she didn't have a car, but maybe she could borrow his truck and check a few of the hotels on her own. There had to be some other place she could stay.

Because going to Logan's wasn't an option.

Three

"There it is." Melissa pointed out a road off the highway to Rick as they passed a small country food market that had long closed for the day.

He put on his blinker and made a sharp right turn onto the narrow paved road. In the distance caught beneath the moon's glow, she could just make out a house beyond several fenced pastures.

"So this guy you know has a real ranch?" Rick asked.

"Yeah, it's the real thing." Melissa turned her head away from the window and gave Rick a faint smile. Five years younger than her, he was what women referred to as beautiful—not a common word used to describe a man, but it fitted Rick completely. His black hair was pulled into a ponytail, which accentuated his high cheekbones and gorgeous blue eyes. Surprisingly, he didn't seem to realize how perfectly God had made him. He was a nice person, too, and they shared a great working relationship.

"How do you know him?" he asked, shooting her a glance.

A flash of her past whipped through her mind. "We met at a party when I was twenty." Actually, because she and Logan had gone to the same high school, she'd known who he was. He'd been three years ahead of her and hadn't even known her name. Back then, all the girls had had crushes on Logan Voss.

Except she'd never grown out of hers. A couple of years after graduation they met and began dating and she'd fallen madly in love with him. Ruggedly male and hard-working, he was also as gentle as he was intense, as loving as he was stubborn.

"An old boyfriend?" Rick wiggled his eyebrows suggestively.

"Something like that." An old boyfriend. A former lover. The man she'd planned to marry.

The man who had broken her heart.

Rick slowed the truck to navigate a sharp curve. "So you grew up here?"

"My father was in the service and was transferred to Reese Air Force Base near Lubbock when I was twelve. We passed through Royal on our way there. He liked it here, so he commuted to work. Once I graduated high school I didn't want to move with my parents when they retired to Florida. So I stayed in Royal."

To be near Logan. But she didn't say that.

She'd never forgotten the moment she'd seen him sitting alone at that party. For years she'd admired him from afar, so, gathering her courage, she'd sat beside him and struck up a conversation. They'd spend the remainder of the evening together, then Logan had taken her home.

The instant chemistry between them had led to a heated kiss. A few dates later, with their passion still burning hot, she'd given him her virginity.

Over the next few months, their relationship had grown more intense. And emotional. As a teenager, Melissa had sworn she wouldn't turn out like her mother, a talented dancer who had given up her chance at stardom to become the wife of a career military man and follow him from base to base as he moved up the ranks.

Not her. She had wanted to do so much more.

Until she'd fallen in love with Logan.

For the first time in her life, it all made sense. Love, happiness, being with the man you couldn't live without. Having his children. Growing old with him.

She'd wanted all those things with Logan so much that she'd tossed away her dreams of leaving Royal and becoming a reporter.

Logan had asked her to marry him.

Melissa sighed just thinking about how happy she'd been at that very moment. "Yes," she'd whispered. And Logan had kissed her tenderly. Then he held her in his arms and said, "I'll have everything I've ever wanted, Melissa. I'll have you and the Wild Spur."

It hadn't occurred to her that it might be an unusual thing to say at all. He'd always loved the ranch. But the next day she'd learned from a casual friend the cold truth of why Logan had asked her to marry him—a far cry from his whispered words of love.

The truck traveled over the cattle guard, jarring Melissa out of her thoughts. Her stomach felt like lead as they drove under the Wild Spur entrance and up the long drive to the main house. She stared out the window, mesmerized by how the landscape had changed. Three cottages dotted a circular drive she couldn't recall. Next to them, the trees had flourished, blocking their view of the main house.

Several outbuildings lay to her right, each very large and well-kept. Beyond them in the distance stood an impressive row of stables and several large corrals. Progress and improvements had changed the small ranch she'd known into a major, thriving business.

The truck rounded a small curve and at the sight of Logan's home, she caught her breath. It barely resembled the small, functional ranch house she'd remembered.

Pulling into a driveway of cocoa-colored stone, Rick stopped his truck in front of a grand courtyard enclosed with an equally impressive stone wall. A majestic fountain stood like a monument in the center of it, welcoming them.

She opened her door, climbed out of the truck and her stomach knotted tighter as she took in the massive house. Although she recognized a part of the original building, the majority of it had clearly been constructed since she'd left town.

It was, in a word…stunning.

The Spanish-style house boasted a low-pitched terracotta roof, rounded windows and stucco walls painted a pale shade of peach. An array of native foliage gave the iron-gated entryway and courtyard lushness, as did the beautiful flagstone patio and walkway.

It seemed Logan's management of the ranch had paid off nicely. He'd always been devoted to this place, she thought with a sense of resignation—enough to marry her to acquire it. Obviously he'd succeeded in getting the ranch, despite the fact that she'd refused to be used as a ticket to secure his heritage.

Had he and his brother Bart struck another deal of some kind, or had one of them married to lock down their legacy? What had happened to Bart? she wondered.

The brothers had had little in common. Unlike Logan, Bart, a few years younger, had hated living in the country, raising cattle and handling horses. Though Melissa hadn't thought he'd been a bad seed, he'd found his way into his share of trouble. Aware Logan's father had favored Bart, Melissa once had asked Logan why.

He'd told her that their mother had died of cancer when he was eleven and Bart was six. At first, Bart had withdrawn, then later he became difficult to handle. His father had tried to compensate for his distress by giving into his demands. Logan hadn't expressed bitterness or jealousy; he'd simply accepted his father's obvious favoritism without complaining. Or showing emotion.

What had happened between the two brothers since she'd left? Had Bart followed through with his plans to leave Royal for good when he got his share of his inheritance?

Following Rick to the back of his truck, she retrieved

her bag, which held little more than her makeup and one change of clothing. Having tailed them from the celebration, Daniel parked his car behind Rick's truck in the wide driveway. Melissa waited as he got out and joined them.

When she'd agreed to this assignment, it had been with Daniel's assurance that they'd only be in Royal for an overnight stay. No longer.

And surely not as long as it would take to do a series of feature stories on Royal.

Disgruntled at the turn of events, she debated letting someone else approach Logan's door, then decided if she acted as though something was bothering her, it would make her coworkers more curious about her relationship with him. And after the way she and Logan had disappeared from the ball, the last thing she wanted to do was to give either Daniel or Rick anything additional to talk about.

As she started toward the house, the door opened and Logan walked out. He was followed by a short, stout woman with rosy cheeks and a smile big enough to win over Snow White's dwarf, Grumpy.

"I see you made it," Logan commented, centering his gaze on Melissa as he greeted the group. "This is Norah Campbell. Officially, she's the housekeeper, but she's really the boss. She keeps the place running smoothly."

Norah gave Logan a fond look, then smiled widely at them. "Welcome to the Wild Spur. We're pleased to have you stay with us. We want you to feel right at home, so if there's anything you need, please let me know."

Melissa extended her hand and shook Norah's. "Hi,

I'm Melissa Mason. This is Daniel Graves and Rick Johnson. We appreciate having a place to stay at the last minute and hope we haven't put you to too much work."

"Not at all. It's nice to meet you. I have your accommodations ready." She nodded to Logan. "Why don't you take the men to their quarters, and I'll show Miss Mason to her room."

"Melissa, please."

"And I'm Norah. Let's go inside. I'm sure you're tired."

As she started to follow Norah inside the house, Melissa heard the groan of a car door opening. Turning back, she saw Rick and Logan get in Rick's truck and Daniel climb in his car. Her heart began to pound as they started their automobiles, then backed out of the driveway. Turning to Norah, she asked, "Where are they going?"

"Logan's taking them to one of the guest cottages. You passed them on the way in. Come, let me show you to your room."

Melissa watched the vehicles drive away, then pull in several hundred yards from the main house.

Why would Logan locate the men in one of the cottages, separating them from her? Did he want her in the main house to corner her? She knew he wanted to talk about why she'd left years ago, but she had no plans to let him have his way. No good could come from revisiting that emotional nightmare.

"Logan thought they'd be more at ease in one of the cottages," Norah added as they went inside. "We talked about having you stay in one as well."

"Why didn't you?" Melissa asked as she took in the breathtaking foyer. Polished wood floors reflected light from a delicate chandelier hanging overhead and an antique grandfather clock stood watch in the corner.

"He thought you'd be more comfortable here in the house."

Melissa didn't believe that for a minute. Logan had always been as tenacious as a pit bull when it came to getting his way. Apparently that was one thing about him that hadn't changed.

As she followed the housekeeper, Melissa found the rest of Logan's house as extraordinary as the foyer. All on one level, it was spread out, easily more than five thousand square feet. When they neared the living room, Norah stopped and Melissa stared in awe at its richness. Wide framed windows, a large flagstone fireplace and soft leather furniture gave it a comfortable, yet luxurious feel.

"This is beautiful. Everything looks so different."

"So you've been here before?" Norah asked.

Melissa realized her blunder and forced a smile. "It was a long time ago. How long have you worked for Logan?"

Norah led them down another hallway. "I moved here about eight years ago. My husband passed away and my sister lives nearby and wanted me close to her. I was happy to get a job here. Logan was in need of help and I needed something to do."

"So you enjoy working for him?" Melissa asked.

The housekeeper smiled. "Oh, I do. I wouldn't want to work anywhere else."

"He's fortunate to have you," Melissa commented.

Norah shook her head. "I'm the lucky one. I never had children so I think of Logan as my son."

Curious to learn a little more about him, Melissa asked, "Is he difficult to work for?"

"Oh, quite the opposite."

"Really?" She couldn't stop herself from pumping the housekeeper for more information.

"He's awfully quiet sometimes and doesn't go out much. I worry that he's never going to find the right woman and settle down."

Melissa followed Norah into a bedroom and put her bag on the floor. Did Norah's comment mean that Logan had never brought a woman here? She couldn't help being curious about his past. She walked over to the bed and ran her finger along one of the fluffy pillows.

"How lovely." The cherry furniture was simple, yet elegant, the queen-size bed covered in a beautiful comforter of burgundy, teal and gold that matched the long drapes at the windows. Iron wall sconces with candles burned a delicate scent of vanilla throughout the room. She looked at the older woman. "Did you decorate it?"

Norah shook her head. "Heavens, no."

"The room definitely has a woman's touch," she commented.

"Logan hired a decorator to redo the entire house. He didn't want anything here to remind him of his ex-wife."

Melissa's gaze snapped to Norah's. "*His ex-wife?* Logan was married?" she asked, breathless.

"Only for about a year from what I've heard. He

doesn't mention her very often, well, truthfully, pretty much never."

"When was he married?"

"I believe he got divorced about ten years ago."

Logan had married someone else.

Pain sliced through her. That meant he'd met and married someone shortly after she'd left Royal. Or worse, was he seeing someone else when he was dating her?

Oh, God.

Balling her hands into fists, Melissa fought back waves of heartache. He hadn't loved her after all. He'd wanted this ranch desperately enough to ask *her* to marry him. When she'd left, he hadn't wasted time finding another woman to take her place.

She'd always thought that she'd been right about Logan's motives for proposing, but over the years doubts had plagued her. Having her beliefs confirmed shouldn't have hurt her, but it did.

The bastard!

Who was the woman he'd married? Where had he met her? And more importantly, when?

"I hope you'll be comfortable here. The bathroom is through there. It's completely furnished with toiletries, but if you need anything at all, please press this button." She pointed to an elaborate intercom system on the wall.

"Thank you." Numb, Melissa watched Norah leave. All Melissa wanted was this night to be over. And to sleep. Tomorrow would be a long, difficult day. She'd need her wits about her when she saw Logan again.

If he continued to pressure her, she had a few questions for him—ones she was sure he wouldn't want to answer.

She wasn't too sure she wanted to hear what he had to say, either.

Setting her bag on the bed, she searched through it for the clothes she'd worn during the day—a pair of black slacks and a blue silk blouse. She'd need to wear those tomorrow. Perhaps the first order of business in the morning would be shopping for some clothes and shoes.

Spotting her nightgown, she pulled it out and tossed it across a pillow. Restless, she paced across the room and glanced out the window. Her room was situated at the front of the house and she could clearly see the nearby cottages. Why had he chosen to install her in his home?

To embarrass her? To make her feel uncomfortable? Well, he'd accomplished both.

Feeling edgy, Melissa walked over to the bed. At this rate she wasn't going to get an ounce of sleep. She needed a book or a newspaper, something to take her mind off seeing Logan again, sleeping in his house. Then she remembered seeing some magazines in his living room when she'd passed it earlier. Hoping she could find the way, she went in search of it.

A few minutes after leaving her room, she'd gotten turned around and wasn't even sure where the living room was, but she passed by what looked to be Logan's study and noticed a few magazines on a table. Stepping inside, she picked one up and thumbed through it. She was turning to leave when she was startled by Logan's voice.

"I didn't expect to see you again until morning."

Melissa dropped the magazine to the floor. "I'm sorry. I didn't realize you were in here." He must have been sitting in his chair with his back to her. Darn!

Logan watched her pick up the magazine and straighten. "Somehow I figured out on my own that you hadn't come looking for me."

"I couldn't sleep, no thanks to you."

Logan stood. "You're annoyed."

Fire flashed through her eyes. Annoyed? No, she was angry that he'd professed to love her, only to marry another woman shortly after she'd left. "I don't like being manipulated."

"All I did was offer you and your coworkers a place to stay." Despite Melissa's terse tone, Logan couldn't take his eyes off her. Even mad at him, she was beautiful. He'd dreamed of seeing her again, but he'd never allowed himself to believe she might one day be in his house. To have her here brought a wealth of emotions to the surface. Frustration. Hurt. Anger.

And desire.

She clutched the magazine to her. "Don't, Logan."

"Don't what, sweetheart?" he asked, shoving his hands in his pockets.

"Make light of what you've done."

"Meaning?"

"Using our situation of being without a hotel room to install me in your house. Or should we start where you approached me at the ball? Take your pick," she told him, still angry with him.

Logan walked over to her. "I thought I was doing you a favor."

She held up her hand. "It won't work. You're not going to make me feel guilty about leaving."

He stepped closer until only inches separated them. "You're the one who brought it up this time, Melissa. Maybe you do feel guilty. Care to talk about it?"

"No." At his nearness, Melissa swallowed hard. He was too near. Too dangerous. Too tempting. She stepped back. "I think I better leave."

"Really?" he murmured, his voice hoarse. Logan closed the distance between them and slipped his hand behind her neck, his fingers inching into her hair. He wondered how, after she'd left him, he could feel anything more than pain. But he couldn't deny that he wanted to kiss her.

Melissa pressed her hands against his chest. "Yes." She lifted her face to his, stared into his eyes, refused to back down.

"Did you ever think about me, about what we had together?"

Sensations of awareness coiled through her as he watched her, his gaze intense. "No."

"You're lying." Logan ran his thumb over her bottom lip, wanting more than ever to taste her. But he'd be foolish to get involved with her again. She'd proven to him once that she couldn't be trusted with his heart. "When the time is right, you'll admit it. I can promise you that." With every ounce of willpower he had, he let her go and went to the door.

"Logan." Melissa waited for him to look at her. When he did, her knees went weak even as her confidence returned. "Don't push me," she said boldly. "You might not like what you hear."

Without answering, he walked out, leaving her wondering what would have happened if he'd kissed her. Would kissing him have proven that she was over him? Or, God forbid, would it have reawakened feelings for him she'd buried deep inside?

She began to pace. How was she going to stay in his house and be able to keep her emotions under lock and key? Every time he came near her, every time he touched her, she wanted to know what it would be like to taste him again. The longer she stayed, the more difficult it would be to keep him at arm's length.

And that's what she wanted, no *needed,* to do.

As Melissa returned to her room and put on her nightgown, she decided that tomorrow she'd focus on gathering information for her story. Once she covered all aspects of it, she'd leave Royal, and Logan, behind.

This time forever.

In his bedroom, Logan stripped off his clothes and took a cold shower. It did little to take his mind off the woman sleeping across the hall. Having Melissa walk back into his life had disrupted his otherwise placid life.

He was the one who had orchestrated getting her here to his home so if he lost a night's sleep obsessing about her, he had only himself to blame. What *had* he been thinking? Their past relationship and subsequent breakup should have warned him to stay away from her.

When she'd broken up with him and left town, he'd been hurt and disappointed and disheartened. She'd never given him the chance to talk to her. Why? He'd been foolish enough to believe she loved him. But a better opportunity clearly had come her way and she'd grabbed it without even thinking about him.

He'd been in a well of pain, given to feeling sorry for himself until eventually, feeding on the need to survive without her, he'd pulled himself together enough to think about the ranch.

Then he'd met Cara through his brother, Bart. Attractive and provocative, she'd stroked his ego. Before he knew what hit him, he was knee-deep involved with her. When she began talking about getting married, Logan hadn't taken her seriously because they hadn't been dating very long. But then, he'd thought, he hadn't known Melissa long, either, and he'd wanted to marry her.

But Cara had kept talking about marriage and he warmed to the idea. He cared for her, and they'd enjoyed being with each other.

Though he could honestly say he'd tried, his relationship with Cara hadn't worked out. She hadn't been any happier on the ranch than Bart had been. While Logan and Cara had gotten along well when dating, they'd argued often during their marriage. Finally, Logan hadn't been able to take it any longer. When he'd asked her for a divorce, she hadn't fought him. It was only after she'd left that he'd faced the truth—he hadn't loved her.

Not like Melissa.

Half aroused from thinking about her sleeping across the hall, he threw his damp towel on the bathroom vanity, went into his bedroom and climbed into bed. As he lay down, he interlaced his hands under his head and stared at the ceiling.

Was he a fool to have brought Melissa here? He'd thought he'd been smart by keeping her in town to confront her.

And to give himself peace of mind.

So far, at every turn, instead of putting his past with Melissa to rest, she'd stirred up feelings of frustration, anger and awareness.

And lust.

The sex between them had always run hot, the reason he'd become so deeply involved with her. The first time he made love to her, he'd known that what he felt for her was different than for any other woman he'd been with. She'd gotten under his skin.

Now things were different. When she'd left him before, she'd severed any emotional attachment he'd had for her.

Lust he could handle.

His goal in getting Melissa to stay in Royal wasn't about getting her in bed.

As long as he remembered that, his heart was safe.

Recently elected to the position of sheriff, Gavin O'Neal was well-respected throughout the community. As a member of the TCC, his experience in law enforcement was invaluable. With their property lines next to each other, Gavin and Logan were neighbors as well as friends.

So why was he calling so early?

Dropping into his chair behind his desk, Logan picked up the telephone. "Hey, Gavin."

Gavin's voice drawled across the line, "Morning, Logan."

"What's up?"

"Can you meet at the club this morning?"

At the seriousness of his friend's tone, Logan sat straighter in his chair. "What's going on?"

"I want to discuss the autopsy findings on Jonathan Devlin. As you know, I'm down a few deputies and I may be needing your help with the investigation."

The recent murder of Jonathan Devlin, the town's main historian, had everyone concerned. After falling into a coma, he'd been hospitalized. In the days prior to his death, he'd begun showing signs of improvement and the doctors cautiously had believed he would recover.

Instead, he'd died of a sudden heart attack.

An ornery man, Jonathan hadn't been especially liked by the community. The circumstances of his death were peculiar, so an autopsy had been performed.

"I've already talked to Jake, Thomas and Connor," Gavin said. "I'll call Mark as soon as I hang up with you."

Logan glanced at his planner. "What time do you want us there?"

"Ten-thirty."

"I'll be there." Logan disconnected the line.

Grimacing, he stood and left the study. What had Gavin found? From his hard tone, it couldn't be good.

Logan arrived in the dining room to find Daniel and Rick across from each other at the table already eating.

Rick looked up. "Hi, Logan. We were going to wait for you, but Norah insisted that we start eating while the food was hot."

"I'm glad you did. I had a call I needed to take." He sat at the end of the table nearest them. "Where's Melissa?" Logan hadn't meant to ask, but the words had just spilled out of his mouth. Annoyed with himself, he buttered a piece of toast, then added some eggs and bacon to his plate.

"Haven't seen her yet," Rick said.

Logan raised an eyebrow. When he'd dated her, she usually had been out of bed before him. "Not a morning person?"

"Are you kidding?" Daniel took a sip of his coffee, made a grunt of approval, then took another sip. "She's usually the first one into work every day."

Chewing his food, Logan found that interesting. It could only mean one thing. Melissa *was* in her room avoiding him. Well, if she thought she'd wait him out, she was in for a surprise.

He wasn't going anywhere until he saw her.

The scent of bacon and eggs hit Melissa as she left her room the next morning. The thought of eggs made her stomach roil. She'd settle for a cup of coffee and a piece of toast. She'd hardly slept at all, and she wasn't in the greatest of moods. It had nothing to do with her conversation with Logan last night. Nothing to do with being tempted to kiss him.

Nothing to do with sleeping only a few rooms away from him.

Today she would borrow Daniel's car to run some errands. Before she did any additional investigation on her story, she needed to buy some clothes.

Her steps faltered as she entered the dining room and saw Logan. He was sitting at a large walnut table, a cup of coffee in his hand. Daniel and Rick also were seated at the table.

"Good morning, everyone. I was hoping to find a cup of coffee."

Logan looked up at her approach. "Have a seat. I'll pour you some."

She saw the coffee urn on the table and reached for it. "Thanks, Logan, but please don't get up. I can do it," she said without looking at him.

"Morning, Melissa," Daniel said.

Rick finished a bite of his food, then swallowed. "Hey, Melissa."

With her cup full, she pulled out a chair and sat down, thankful that Rick and Daniel were seated next to Logan and she didn't have to sit near him. She added sugar and cream to her coffee, then looked up at Daniel. "I'd like to borrow your car for a while this morning. I have some errands to run. I also need to head over to the museum and check out the Halifax exhibit, get the details on what happened with the vandalism."

Daniel shook his head. "Sorry, Melissa, but my plans have changed. As much as I was looking forward to staying here for a few days, I have to head back to Houston."

Melissa's hand froze in the middle of reaching for a piece of toast. "What? Why?"

"Jason called this morning. There's a story breaking in Houston about busting a drug ring."

"Then we're leaving," she concluded.

"I am," he clarified. "I'm leaving you and Rick here to work on the Jessamine Golden story and how it might tie in with the Halifax exhibit."

"Are you sure you want to go there, Daniel?" she asked, trying one last time to dissuade him. "There's probably nothing to it. So far, no one even knows what it means. And the map is hardly worth mentioning."

Daniel picked up his cup, then paused before taking a sip. "Stay on it. The appearance of the map is interesting enough to follow. And I want more about the historical mystery." He nodded. "Contact me when you've finished your first segment on the ball and the Halifax exhibit."

Frustrated, she set down her coffee. "I'll work on it. I hope the mystery surrounding Jessamine Golden doesn't disappoint you."

"It's going to go over big. I just know it. A lot of wealthy, influential people live here. Who knows who could be involved?" He sat back in his chair and looked at Logan with gratitude. "Well, I've gotta run. I can't thank you enough for your hospitality, Logan." He stood and extended his hand. "Don't get up. I'll see myself out."

"You're welcome anytime." As Daniel left, Logan

glanced at Melissa, who didn't look at all pleased that her producer was leaving her in Royal. From the cold shoulder she'd been giving him, he had a feeling she was eager to avoid him. More determined than ever to pin her down, he said, "I can give you a lift into town, Melissa." Being alone with her in the car would be the perfect opportunity to question her. She couldn't avoid answering him there.

"I appreciate it, Logan, but Rick will still be here. I'll ride in with him."

Rick stuffed the last of his bacon into his mouth, chewed it, then swallowed. "Logan said I could hang around the ranch this morning and take a look at his operation."

She stared at him with disbelief. "What?"

He shrugged his shoulders. "C'mon, Melissa. You're not going to be shooting this morning, are you?"

"Well, no, but—"

"Then you don't really need me. The ranch foreman's already agreed to let me tag along with him for a while."

"I have a meeting at the Cattleman's Club so I'm going into town anyway," Logan cut in. "You might as well ride with me."

Melissa finished the last of her coffee. This wasn't working at all the way she'd planned. The last thing she wanted was to spend more time in Logan's company. Why? she asked herself. Because she didn't trust Logan? Or because she didn't trust her own feelings for him? "Thanks anyway, but I can take Rick's truck."

"If you take my truck, then later want me to meet you, I won't have any way to get there," Rick told her.

"All right," she said, accepting her fate. "But keep your cell phone with you in case I need you." Fine. She'd ride into town with Logan. Maybe after she poked around a little at the museum, she'd learn that the vandalism of the exhibit was merely a prank. If so, she'd write a conclusion to her story and leave Royal by tomorrow.

And say goodbye to Logan. Again.

Logan's pickup rocked as he hit a pothole on the back road before turning onto the main highway and heading toward Royal. "Do you plan to remain silent the entire ride?" He glanced at Melissa. "Or do you plan to talk to me?"

Melissa looked up from her reporter's notebook. "I'm not ignoring you. I'm thinking about the story I'm working on." She went back to flipping through the pages. If she were inclined to talk, she'd demand to know who he'd married. Which she could never do because it would seem as if she were interested in him. Which she wasn't. Really.

Still, it grated on her nerves to know he'd married within months of her leaving. His actions only solidified her reason for breaking up with him. He'd needed a wife to secure his inheritance. It hadn't mattered who the woman was.

Old hurt coiled through her as she recalled the day she'd found out why he'd proposed. She'd run into a friend from school, Cara Young, who had been dating Logan's brother, Bart. Cara had revealed that the terms of their father's will dictated that the first of his sons to marry would inherit the ranch.

Because he didn't want the ranch, Bart had refused to marry Cara to get it. He'd told her that he and Logan had made a deal. Logan would marry Melissa, thereby securing the ranch, then he'd buy out Bart's portion. Cara had been furious.

Crushed and betrayed, Melissa hadn't wanted to believe Cara. But she'd thought about Logan's words right after he'd proposed.

I'll have everything I've ever wanted, Melissa. I'll have you and the Wild Spur.

The truth had been right there for her to hear. She had been too in love with Logan to see it. So she'd done the only thing she could to save her self-respect. She'd given Logan his ring back and left town, using her desire to be a reporter as the reason she'd changed her mind about marrying him.

Did he really want to dredge all that up?

Glancing at him, Melissa noticed his taut jaw, his white knuckles as he gripped the steering wheel. This certainly wasn't going to be a pleasant experience if they couldn't be civil with each other. She'd probably be with him for only a few days at the most. How hard could it be?

"I appreciate your giving me a lift into town."

"Where do you want to go first?" Logan asked, deciding not to press her now. They'd be in town in a few minutes. When he talked to her, he wanted time on his side.

"Shopping."

Her response evoked a grin from him and lightened his mood as he thought about the times they'd gone shopping together. "You always did like clothes." And she'd looked damn good in whatever she wore. Even better when she was naked. He stole a look at her, letting his gaze drift over her breasts. Though she was still thin, her body had gentle curves and swells that were hard to ignore. He dragged his eyes back to the road.

"I can't very well wear these same clothes every day that I'm here," she said, feeling the need to defend herself because he probably hadn't forgotten how much she loved shopping. He used to go with her often.

"I was just teasing you."

"Oh, gee, I missed that."

"You can walk around naked for all I care."

Her eyes widened. "Logan!"

Thinking about her naked sent all kinds of erotic images through his mind. Ever since she'd arrived, Logan had been fighting the desire to kiss her. Though he'd started this, he needed to clear his thoughts. Otherwise he would be very uncomfortable for the remainder of the ride into town—and the rest of the day. "All right. Do you want to go to the museum after you shop?"

She watched him warily. "Yes. I think that's the best place to start investigating the vandalism of the Halifax exhibit."

"I don't know how long my meeting will be. I'll drop you downtown, then come back and pick you up."

"Thanks." She turned to a fresh page in her notebook and jotted down her phone number, then she ripped out the page and handed it to him. "This is my cell number. Call me when you're on your way and I'll let you know where I am."

He stuffed it into his front shirt pocket. "I shouldn't be too long."

She turned a little in her seat to face him. "As a longtime resident, why do you think anyone would vandalize the Halifax exhibit?"

He shrugged. "Beats me. Maybe someone's just trying to tarnish Gretchen Halifax's name. Could be someone doesn't want her to win against Jake for mayor," he speculated.

Her brows dipped in thought. "Do you think she *will* win?"

"It's hard to say. Jake is a strong candidate. He's a local businessman and he's well liked in the community."

By his tone, Melissa read into what he hadn't said. "And Gretchen Halifax isn't?"

"I didn't say that, but, truthfully, I don't know her that well. She comes across as very ambitious. I guess that's not always a bad thing."

Intrigued, Melissa jotted some notes on her pad. "Does she have any secrets?"

"None that I know of." He had a gut feeling there was more to her, but with nothing solid to go on, he didn't speculate further.

"Does Jake Thorne?"

At her focused, intelligent questions, Logan let his gaze drifted over her feminine features. She was a beautiful woman, but he'd always known there was more to Melissa than her appearance.

He looked back at the road as he turned onto the street leading to the center of town. "No. He's running against Gretchen because he feels her platform on tax reform may have a negative effect on local businesses in Royal."

"What about you? Do you think Jake is a better candidate for mayor, or as a businessman, is he protecting his own interests?" Melissa knew he was one of Logan's close friends. Did his loyalty to Jake make him blind to his flaws?

Logan's mouth tightened. "Jake is as upstanding as you get."

Melissa had to stop herself from grinning. Obviously she was right. Jake was Logan's friend, and Logan was loyal to a fault.

Except with you.

Melissa tamped down on her feelings of resentment and tried to keep her focus on her story. "I wasn't suggesting that he wasn't," she replied, softening her tone. "I'm just trying to find out what's going on."

"Right." Just like he was trying to find out why she'd left. And eventually he would. He just hoped he wouldn't be sorry when he did. He tabled his thoughts as he pulled up to a curb in the upscale shopping district. "My meeting shouldn't take more than an hour or two."

She reached for her door handle. "I'll be ready when you are."

"You don't have to rush."

"Thanks." Melissa got out of the truck, then gave him a wave. Maybe she didn't have to rush shopping, but she did have to rush to get this story done so she could return to her life in Houston.

So far today she'd avoided any further personal discussions with Logan. She didn't expect her luck would hold out, though, not with the looks she'd been getting from him. Or the innuendos.

Still, the question of his marriage burned in her mind. Maybe talking with him would be worth the pain if she forced him to admit the truth. Maybe she'd leave Royal this time with her mind clear of Logan Voss.

And her heart.

Logan pulled to a stop in the parking lot of the Texas Cattleman's Club just as Connor Thorne, Jake's brother, got out of his car. Unlike Jake, who was outgoing and easy to know, Connor was on the quiet side. Though his hair was cut short the way he'd worn it when he'd served as an army Ranger, he'd resigned his commission to return home and run the family's engineering business. Connor didn't talk about his reasons, but Logan suspected something had happened to cause him to give up his chosen career.

"Hey, Connor," Logan called as he got out of his truck and met him in front of the club. They exchanged pleasantries, then Logan said, "It looks like Jake, Mark and Tom Morgan have already arrived." He gestured toward their vehicles.

Connor nodded. "Yeah. Now we're only waiting for Gavin."

Together they entered the club and went to a private room in the rear. Moments later, Gavin walked in and everyone but the sheriff seated themselves around the large conference table.

"I'm glad you all could make it," Gavin stated. He took off his hat and dropped it on the table. He looked at every man in the room, his gaze pausing briefly on each. "Since I'm down a few deputies I could use your help."

"Anything we can do," Logan said. The rest of the men voiced their agreement.

"As you know, Jonathan Devlin was murdered." All of the men nodded. "Until I made headway into the investigation, I've kept the results of the autopsy confidential, even from the family, because I don't know who was involved."

"And now?" Logan asked.

"The investigation is snowballing."

Jake was the one who asked the question on all of their minds. "So how was Jonathan Devlin killed?"

Gavin released a sigh. "Lethal injection."

"What was in it?" Tom asked, leaning forward.

Logan understood Tom's interest. Recently, Tom had learned that Jonathan was his great-grandfather. Adopted at birth, it wasn't until after his mother died that Tom had returned to Royal in search of his family.

Meeting Jonathan must have been an eye-opener. The man had had a reputation of being difficult and he'd ruled his family with an iron fist. There was no telling who had murdered him.

"Potassium chloride," Gavin told them. "Which is why it looked as though he died of cardiac arrest."

"Did they find any needle marks on him?" Connor asked.

The sheriff tapped his fingers on the table. "No. We believe it was given to him through his intravenous drip."

"Then the killer got to him in the hospital." Logan voiced what they were all thinking.

"That's a fair assumption, but so far there's no proof. My main focus at this time is hospital staff members, anyone who has worked there in the past year and family members who could have had a grudge against him."

"Do you have any leads?" Tom asked.

Gavin sighed. "More than my men and I can handle. I don't like the idea of a killer running loose in our town. We're following up the leads as quickly as we can."

Jake rested his elbows on the conference table. "How about suspects?"

Gavin pulled out a chair, turned it around and straddled it. "No one solid. I went out to Jonathan's house, but found nothing significant to his murder."

"Anything else?" Logan asked.

"Not yet. We're still analyzing evidence and hoping something will turn up to lead us to the killer."

"What about one of the Windcrofts?" Jake asked. "They've been fighting with the Devlins for more than a hundred years over whether Nicholas Devlin cheated Richard Windcroft out of half of his land in a poker game."

"But their feud has never led to murder," Connor reasoned out loud.

"Except when Nicholas was shot," Tom offered. "My family still talks about it. They believe a Windcroft was responsible."

"But why would a Windcroft want Jonathan dead?" Gavin asked. "What would they gain?" He shook his head. "I don't know. It just doesn't add up."

Mark crossed his arms over his chest. "Okay, let's take this in another direction. What about the appearance of the map? Jonathan lived in the same house as Jessamine Golden did. If someone really believes she engineered a gold heist, they might have been after something in the house."

Connor nodded. "Like the map."

"But the map only turned up when Opal Devlin began cleaning out Jonathan's things," Logan pointed out.

Tom rubbed his knuckles against his chin. "Maybe someone already knew about the map's existence."

"Say someone *was* after it," Mark speculated. "Without knowing if the map is authentic, who would want it bad enough to kill Jonathan?"

Connor sat forward. "How about Malcolm Durmorr?" he suggested. "He's related to the Devlins, but he's never been welcomed into the family fold and he's been on the wrong side of the law more than once."

"Could be him, but hell, with the map made public and on display at the museum, it could be anyone who believes it might lead to a treasure of gold bars. There's something else." Logan dreaded this part because he knew his friends were going to get on his case about a reporter staying at his ranch. "Melissa Mason, the reporter from WKHU in Houston, is staying at my ranch and is doing a story on Royal's celebration and history. She's planning to mention the map in her feature. When it airs, every kook within a thousand-mile radius will be after it."

"Another reason I need your help," Gavin stated. "As I've said, the Devlin murder case is keeping me busy. Aaron Hill at the Heritage Society Museum would like some assistance safeguarding the map. I suggested the TCC handle the duty since my department is short on manpower. Can I count on you to keep the map secure and do some discreet investigating on Jonathan's murder? Use your own contacts and report back to me if you find anything that could be connected to it."

Logan nodded. "You got it."

Tom gave Logan a contemplative look. "Melissa Mason is quite a looker. How are you standing it having her under your roof?"

Jake chuckled. "Yeah, Logan. Hell, I want to know how you managed to get her out to your ranch."

"If I'd known she needed a place to sleep, I would have offered her a bed," Connor stated, then quipped, *"Mine."*

All of the men laughed—except Logan. He didn't find Connor's comment amusing. The thought of Connor sleeping with Melissa irked him. "She's not available."

At his gruff tone, Mark's eyebrows shot up. "Oh, is that the way the wind blows?"

"Don't go reading anything into it. She's planning to return to Houston as soon as she finishes her report here." Logan stood, cutting off any further discussion about Melissa. "When Gavin has more news, we'll meet back here and discuss any action we need to take. In the meantime, let's keep a watch out for anything unusual."

Five

Having called Melissa to let her know he was on his way, Logan pulled up to the curb in front of the same department store where he'd left her. Though he'd told her not to rush, she'd assured him she'd finished shopping and was ready.

As he opened his truck door and got out, he spotted her walking toward him, her arms loaded with packages of all shapes and sizes, several full shopping bags hanging from her hands. Walking around the vehicle, he relieved her of most of the packages.

"Have fun?" he asked. It looked as if she'd bought out the store. Logan opened the tailgate and deposited her items inside.

"Actually, yes." Her eyes sparkled with excitement. With her busy schedule, she rarely had time to shop.

More often than not, she would run into a store for a specific item. The couple of hours that Logan had been gone had passed rather quickly, but she was surprised at what she'd managed to buy.

She'd also used the time to put her feelings for Logan into perspective—or rather, to face her attraction to him. It was there every moment he was near her, that breathless feeling of anticipation.

When she'd been young and naive, she'd loved him with all of her heart so it only made sense that she still had feelings for him buried inside. Denying her obvious attraction toward him would only make her stay here harder. From her earlier response to his touch, Logan knew it, too.

What she'd do about them remained to be seen.

Daniel had accused her of being a workaholic. He was right. It was the way she protected herself. Work had provided a perfect excuse not to become involved with the men she'd dated.

Why should she? She'd never felt that rush, that endless excitement that should accompany intimacy.

Because those men hadn't been Logan.

And because Logan had hurt her, she'd been afraid to open her heart to anyone else.

Seeing Logan again stirred up yearnings for him that had lain dormant. Even though she'd promised herself she could handle her attraction to him, with him close enough to touch, her entire body tensed as if bracing itself.

How did he have the power to do that to her after all these years? Disconcerted, she handed the rest of her packages to him and he put them in the truck along with the others.

Closing the tailgate, Logan turned to her. "Ready to go to the museum?"

"Yes, I'm anxious to get a look at the Halifax exhibit." And to get away from him. The man had an effect on her that should be outlawed.

"Melissa—" Logan started, then heard someone call his name and straightened. He saw Gretchen Halifax coming across the street toward them, her stride purposeful. Though not especially pleased to see her, he was grateful she'd interrupted his errant thought of acting on his attraction to Melissa.

"Hello, Logan," Gretchen said, stopping in front of them. "It's good to see you." She shifted toward Melissa with an engaging smile.

"This is Councilwoman Gretchen Halifax," Logan said by way of an introduction. "Gretchen, Melissa Mason. She's a reporter from Houston. She's doing a series of reports on Royal's anniversary."

"It's nice to meet you," Melissa said, shaking Gretchen's hand. Impeccably dressed from head to toe, Gretchen projected a professional image that few could find fault with. Melissa had noticed the councilwoman last night at the celebration gala. She'd intended to strike up a conversation with Gretchen, until Logan had cornered her and thrown her whole night into chaos.

"I'd heard there was a reporter in town. It's a pleasure to meet you. Our town appreciates your interest. Your stories are bound to draw more visitors to boost our economy."

"Thank you."

"Logan, the ball last night was delightful. Miss Mason, I do hope you were there and enjoyed it."

Melissa had a feeling Gretchen knew specifically that she'd attended and was fishing for details of her and Logan's encounter. Few people could have missed the exchange between them on the dance floor and their quick departure from the room. "Yes, I was there with some of my coworkers. We had a wonderful time."

"I'm glad to hear that. We want you to feel right at home here. How long are you going to be in town?"

Smiling politely, Melissa replied, "For a few days."

Irritation touched Gretchen's face, then she quickly recovered and pasted on her smile. "I'd be happy to do an interview with you if you'd like. I'm running for mayor."

"Yes, I know. I'll keep that in mind," Melissa replied, not at all interested in promoting Gretchen Halifax's political ambitions. Obviously Gretchen was trying to cash in on some free publicity. It was rare for Melissa not to like someone on introduction. Gretchen held herself in a regal way, strived to appear cordial, but Melissa's investigative reporting had honed her skill at reading people. The woman's eyes revealed her to be clever and ambitious.

"Great. I'll look forward to hearing from you." Gretchen turned to Logan. "I wanted to talk to you about the map found with Jessamine Golden's saddlebag."

Logan shifted his stance, curious as to why she was interested. "What about it?"

"Do you think it's wise to have the map displayed at the Historical Society Museum indefinitely?"

"It belongs to them, and it's under lock and key," he reminded her.

"Yes, but with what happened to my ancestor's exhibit, it might not be safe there." To Melissa she added, "Edgar Halifax was my great-great uncle, the first mayor of Royal."

Melissa forced a patient smile. "Yes, I know."

"I think it'll be fine," Logan assured Gretchen, but he couldn't help wondering what she was up to. Her concern about the map intrigued him.

Melissa touched Logan's arm. "I was planning to ask if I could use the map for my story, display it where the camera can get a clear shot of it."

With a sniff of disapproval, Gretchen tilted her chin up and gave Melissa a patronizing look. "That's not a good idea, Miss Mason. The map may be valuable. Left out in the open, someone could steal it."

Logan stiffened at Melissa's side. "The director of the museum has asked the members of the Cattleman's Club to safeguard it."

The councilwoman's lips thinned to a line. "I'll be happy to secure it in my safe."

"I'll talk to the members of the club and we'll get back to you, Gretchen, but I don't think that'll be necessary." Logan's tone was firm.

"I'm just trying to help," Gretchen declared, her tone turning slightly brusque.

"And we appreciate it." He gave her a nod. "I'll be in touch."

With a tight smile, Gretchen said goodbye and strode away, her heels tapping sharply on the sidewalk.

Melissa released a slow sigh, then realized she was still holding Logan's arm. He looked at her at that moment, and she pulled away. "Sorry," she mumbled.

He shook his head. "That woman is something else."

"She has quite an overwhelming presence, doesn't she?" Melissa remarked. "Why do you think she was so interested in holding onto the map?"

"No idea," Logan answered. "She could be concerned about preserving the town's history as part of her platform."

"Probably."

He opened the passenger door of his truck and waited for her to get in, then went around and climbed behind the wheel. After merging into traffic, he headed out of town toward the museum.

"How did your meeting go?" she asked, curious to know what he and his friends had talked about at the club. She'd asked around about the Texas Cattleman's Club. Some people had suggested it was a social club where the men could go for conversation and relaxation. But when she'd lived in Royal she'd heard rumors that the club was some sort of secret organization of men who performed dangerous missions, solved crimes and ran rescue operations.

It was a silly notion, of course. It wasn't as though they were superheroes. But she did wonder about Logan's involvement.

"The meeting went fine," Logan replied, not revealing what he'd discussed with his friends. Melissa would find out soon enough about Jonathan's murder. For now, he'd keep it under his hat, use it as leverage to keep her involved in reporting from Royal if she made noises about leaving.

"Really?"

Her inquisitive expression sent a warning to him. "Yes."

"Hmmm."

Not sure he really wanted to know, but curious as to the direction her mind was going, Logan asked, "What's that 'hmm' for?"

"Who else was there?" she asked, ignoring his question.

Logan shrugged. "A few of my friends."

"Such as…" Melissa waited for him to fill her in.

"Jake Thorne and his brother, Connor."

"Jake, who's running for mayor against Gretchen, right?"

"Yes."

"And what does Connor do?"

"He runs his family's engineering firm."

"Ah. And who else was there?"

Studying her, he said, "You sure are full of questions." He began thinking he was treading on dangerous ground. It wouldn't do for Melissa to know too much about the club or its operations. As far as the public was concerned it was an ordinary club.

"Just curious." She smiled.

"Right." The force of her smile hit him all the way to his heart. He'd always loved her shapely mouth, her tempting, kissable lips. After all these years, he still remembered her taste. Hot, sweet—and capable of driving a man to his knees, begging for more.

"I *am* a reporter," she reminded him.

Logan hadn't forgot that. She'd be leaving within a week or so, as soon as she'd finished her story. "From what I've heard you're good one." Her smile grew wider, reminiscent of the younger woman he'd loved.

"Don't try to sidetrack me with a compliment." His comment was interesting. Had he been checking up on her? Or had he seen one of her reports?

He chuckled. "All right. Mark Hartman, who is another rancher and runs a self-defense studio in town, Tom Morgan, who's related to the Devlins and owns a demolition business, and the sheriff."

She raised her eyebrows.

He glanced at her, his expression guarded. "What's that look for?"

"Well, you're a busy rancher, right?"

"Yeah, so what?"

"Yet you sneak off in the middle of the day for some kind of meeting at the Cattleman's Club."

He laughed. "I wasn't sneaking. It's broad daylight."

"You know what I mean. What's going on? Why are you meeting with the sheriff?"

He hesitated, taking a moment to decide how to answer her without raising her suspicions. "Gavin's asked us to help out the sheriff's office for a while. With budget cuts and a hiring freeze, he's down a couple of deputies." That much was the truth.

She considered that. "So why you guys?"

To appease his desire to touch her and to throw her off balance, he reached over and toyed with a silky strand of her hair. "Most of our members have a military background."

At Logan's touch, Melissa struggled not to lose track of their conversation. Though his explanation sounded reasonable, his hesitation before he replied made her suspect he wasn't being totally upfront. She started to ask him another question, but they approached the museum. The parking lot was almost half-full.

As Logan parked, she smiled. "The museum looks the same." It made her feel good to know that some things never changed. As a teenager she'd loved visiting the museum. The large, two-story, stately brick building, once the home of prominent landowners, was adorned with four ornate white columns and an array of beautiful flowers and shrubs.

They walked up the wide steps and through the arched doorway. Inside, two circular stairways with decorative wrought-iron railings led to the second floor. Original wood floors creaked under their footsteps as they climbed the stairs. Antique cases displayed artifacts of Royal's history, and visitors roamed from room to room.

"It's busier than it used to be," Melissa commented.

"The museum has become a landmark in Royal. It's one of the most popular places for tourists to visit."

"That's wonderful." She looked around, then turned back toward him. "Do you know where the Halifax exhibit is?"

"This way. Both the Halifax Exhibit and Jessamine Golden's items are on display in the gallery up here." At the top of the stairs, Logan guided her to a large room framed by two arched entrances.

She stood in the middle of the room and turned a complete circle. "This will be the perfect place to do a video." Pointing to the black, iron, Western-style chandelier hanging from the ceiling, she nodded. "And there's plenty of light from the chandelier. I'll have Rick check it out, but I believe this will work nicely. All I'll need is a podium to set the map on."

Her excitement over her job drew his attention. She loved what she did. It showed in her eyes, in her voice when she spoke. She'd already said she was up for a promotion. Melissa was going places, had her career planned out, it seemed.

"This way," he said, his mind sizzling like hot pavement. He showed her the Halifax Exhibit first. "Looks like the vandalism has been removed."

"This exhibit will be barely worth mentioning if I don't have any evidence of the damage."

"Aaron Hill, the museum director, may have some pictures and Gavin may have some crime shots, as well."

"Great. I'd like to see if the sheriff will release copies of the photos to me to include in my report."

They moved to Jessamine Golden's display. "Look at the roses tooled on her saddlebag, Logan," she said quietly. A sense of sadness overcame her that she couldn't explain.

Logan reacted to the trace of wistfulness in her tone. "From what I've heard, the rose was her trademark."

"It must have been. It's on the handles of her guns, too." She drew a quick breath, her heart not quite steady. "And there are rose petals from her purse." Dried petals in muted colors of purple and pink lay scattered about the small, antique purse. "A woman who could shoot and was considered an outlaw, yet she kept rose petals."

Meeting Logan's eyes, her gaze softened at the sentimentality. "The roses must have been from someone she loved." Running her fingers across the glass protecting the items, she ached for the outlaw, a woman who also possessed a soft heart.

Logan reached over and touched her shoulder. "You think so?"

Reeling from his touch, Melissa felt heat rush to her cheeks. "I can't explain it. I just feel it inside." She struggled to maintain her distance from Logan. Clearing her throat, she focused on the display to get her bearings. "Do you think the map is authentic?"

"Authentic is one thing, but accurate is another." Not wanting to, but knowing he should, Logan removed his hand from her shoulder. "The markings are unusual and difficult to understand. It may be useless."

"Unless someone figures it out and uses it to find the treasure."

He shrugged. "Anything's possible."

Studying it, Melissa sighed. "Look at all the hearts on it."

Logan leaned over the display case, which brought him within inches of her. Her gentle lilac fragrance drifted to him, shifting his already active libido into high gear. He steeled himself to ignore his body's urges. If he touched her now, he might do something reckless, such as kiss her the way he'd been wanting to since he'd seen her at the ball. "Yeah," he replied, aware his voice wasn't as steady as he'd like. "But it's anyone's guess as to what the hearts mean."

"It's an interesting design, as if Jessamine made sure

she was the only one who could decipher it." Melissa turned toward him. "Look, Logan, I know I have no right to ask a favor, but with your association with the Cattleman's Club, apparently you have some influence. I really want to use the map in my story."

"When do you think you'll be ready to shoot it?"

"In the next day or so. Do you think you can arrange it?"

Logan shoved his hands in his pockets. "Depends."

"On what?"

"What do I get in return?"

Wary, her eyes narrowed. "What do you want?"

His jaw set, he stared her straight in the eyes. "The truth, Melissa. Why did you leave me?"

Gritting her teeth, she sighed heavily. "That's not fair. You're putting this on a personal level."

Logan shrugged as if he didn't care what she thought. "No one ever said life was fair. You want the map. That's my offer. Take it or leave it."

It took Melissa several seconds to calm down before she could speak. When she did, she surprised herself. "All right." She'd tell him what he wanted to know. But what would happen when she did? Was it possible that she'd been wrong to believe Cara? No, she told herself. Logan himself had confirmed what Cara had told her.

Melissa couldn't have been wrong.

"I'll see what I can do," Logan said, pleased with himself.

"Thanks. I'm going to find the museum director, set up a time to meet with him and ask for permission to film here. I'll be right back."

Logan watched her walk away, mesmerized by the sway of her hips. He sighed. Whether it would bring relief or anguish, finally he'd get what he wanted from her.

They decided to double back to town and stop at the Royal Diner for lunch. Logan had to twist Melissa's arm because she'd wanted to head straight to the ranch and start working on her story. So he'd used hunger as a diversion to keep her with him a while longer.

Foolish, he knew. He was kidding himself. The more time he spent with her, the more he wanted to be with her. Though she'd broken his heart, it was as if the years she'd been gone had melted away. The attraction between them still sizzled. Had all of the work he'd done to get her out of his system been for nothing? He needed peace of mind, not complications.

And Melissa had *complication* written all over every inch of her luscious body.

As they were approaching the door of the diner, Logan was surprised to see Lucas Devlin, a local rancher, leaving.

"Hello, Lucas." Logan shook his hand. He'd deemed Lucas, Jonathan's grandson, as the peacekeeper of the Devlin clan. When trouble started brewing between the Devlins and the Windcrofts, Lucas was the one always willing to listen to both sides of the argument. With good sense and a cool head, he attempted to calm down his family.

"Hi, Logan. How are you?"

"Doing fine. How about you?"

Lucas nodded. "Can't complain."

Logan touched Melissa's arm, then slid his hand behind her back, drawing her forward. "This is Melissa Mason. She's a reporter from Houston. They're doing a story on Royal. Melissa, Lucas Devlin."

Melissa smiled. "Hello. It's nice to meet you."

"The pleasure's mine, Miss Mason." A muscle worked in Lucas's jaw. He turned to Logan. "I hate to keep you if you're busy, but I'd like a few minutes of your time."

"Sure," Logan replied. "What can I do for you?"

"I'm concerned about my grandfather's autopsy findings."

At the sparkle of interest in Melissa's eyes, Logan suggested she have a seat and he'd join her in a few minutes.

Melissa nodded. "Yes, of course."

After Melissa left them, he turned to Lucas. "So word of the autopsy has already reached your family," Logan stated. Gavin's investigation at the hospital must have started rumors flying. It didn't take long for news to travel in the town of Royal.

Lucas nodded. "Now that the autopsy is in, we know he was murdered, but we haven't been told how it happened. Since he was in the hospital, I assume it took place there, but I don't know for sure. I wanted to know if you've heard anything else."

Gavin had made it clear that he wasn't ready to release the autopsy findings to anyone, including the family, until he investigated the circumstances further. Unable to tell Lucas what he'd learned, Logan replied evasively, "There's nothing I can tell you that the sheriff hasn't. He's actively investigating the murder."

Lucas put his hand on his hip. “My family’s upset and rightly so.”

“Gavin will get to the bottom of things.”

“I hope so. He was out to my place asking questions, but said he didn’t have anything concrete as yet.”

“These things take a while. Be patient and give it some time.“

Lucas nodded reluctantly. “All right. Well, I’ll let you be on your way.” He settled his hat on his head and walked away.

Logan joined Melissa at their table. One glance at her and he could read the questions in her eyes.

Melissa tilted her head with determination. “Okay, what was that all about?”

Six

"Lucas?"

"Yes." Melissa studied Logan with interest. "I get the feeling you know something. Want to fill me in?"

"Let me ask you a question. Do you have enough information for your story?"

"Not yet. I have to work on the Jessamine Golden angle, then compile my notes. Rick and I will come back into town over the next couple of days and go to the library to research the history of the town and the legend of Jessamine, then go to the museum. I still have to interview Aaron Hill."

"And then what?"

She shrugged. "Daniel wants more on Jessamine and the map. Do you know something that's connected to the investigation that you're not telling me?" she asked pointedly, picking up on his elusiveness.

As a reporter, she suspected Logan knew more than he was admitting. As a woman, she hoped he wasn't. If she finished the story in a few days without another lead, she could leave by the end of the week.

For her, it was easier not living in the past. She'd put her love for Logan under lock and key in her heart. It frightened her to think of opening that box. Because leaving Logan while loving him had been the hardest thing she'd ever done.

"I see." Logan thought about that. Although Daniel had assigned her to work on the mystery aspects of the map and the vandalism of the Halifax exhibit, Logan was sure she would try to leave Royal as soon as she could.

Too bad. He was just as determined to see that she stayed. "I may have something that will keep you here a while longer."

Melissa looked at him, her expression serious. "Okay, you've got my attention." All of her journalistic instincts kicked into high gear. Something was definitely going on with the Devlin murder case and Logan was in on it, which probably was related to his secret meeting at the Cattleman's Club this morning. Which was another subject she'd like to investigate. What exactly was that club all about?

"Off the record?"

"All right. Off the record."

"You know about how Jessamine apparently stole that gold, then disappeared, right?"

"Yes, we've talked about that."

He leaned toward her, propped his elbows on the table and folded his arms. "Well, there have been more recent developments than what I told you." Logan relayed the facts Gavin had given him. "Valid or not, someone seems to believe the map leads to the gold, someone who seems willing to kill for it." These new details definitely added to the mystery of Jessamine Golden.

"Why do you think Jonathan didn't use the map himself to look for the treasure?" Melissa asked.

"We don't know that he wasn't doing that. Maybe that's what got him killed," he suggested.

"That's possible. This definitely adds a twist to the story. If there's a killer on the loose, I want to continue investigating."

Logan should have been happy that he'd manipulated Melissa into staying in Royal, but the way she'd said *investigating* made him uneasy. He gave her a stern look. "I don't want you out asking questions that could get you hurt or, worse, killed."

Finding his statement humorous, she bit her lip to keep from laughing. "That's ridiculous, Logan. I'm an investigative reporter. This is what I do for a living."

A muscle worked in his jaw. "I'm not doubting your experience, but until we know what's going on here, you're not going to stick your neck out. Whoever's behind the murder has proven they'll stop at nothing to get what they want."

Her green eyes narrowed. "You can't stop me."

"I don't intend to. I know you have to do your job. But wherever you go, I go," he told her, his tone resolute.

Melissa frowned. "I don't need you watching over me."

His gaze drifted over her. The problem was he liked watching over her. Too much. "Are you ready to order?"

he asked, changing the subject. When she nodded, he signaled the waitress. As Melissa set the menu aside, the fabric of her silk blouse stretched tightly over her breasts, defining them, teasing his imagination.

Yeah, he wanted her, plain and simple. But this time if anything happened between them, she'd be a sweet diversion while she was in town.

He wasn't looking for anything except a good time.

Later, as they drove back to his ranch, Logan stole a glance at Melissa while she talked about her work. He was struck once again by her beauty and the way her eyes darkened with passion telling him about the stories she'd done. She was sharp, intuitive and persistent.

And sexy as hell.

How would it feel to have all that sexual power focused on him?

By settling her in at his ranch, all he'd done was manage to torture himself. He didn't want to be attracted to her, but from the way his heart squeezed whenever he thought of her, he couldn't deny that he felt something akin to what they had shared years ago.

And that was the crux of his problem.

He didn't love her.

No, his feelings had nothing to do with love. Hell, he'd loved her before and it had only brought him heartache. And that was when she'd been young and pretty. Now she was beautiful and intelligent and fascinating, everything a man could want in a woman.

Everything *he'd* wanted.

But she wasn't the same woman now. And he wasn't

the same man. For years they'd lived two completely separate lives. Yes, he still found her attractive, but it didn't mean he wanted to do anything about it.

Logan simply wasn't interested in getting hurt again. He wasn't searching for a long-term relationship. If he wanted sex, he knew women willing to go to bed with him without strings attached.

He tightened his hand on the steering wheel. Who was he kidding? He wanted Melissa all right—wanted to touch her, wanted a chance to feel her beneath him, to feel himself inside her.

"Logan?"

Realizing she'd asked him something, he shook his head to clear his thoughts. "Yeah?"

"Where were you?" Melissa asked.

What could he say? That he'd been fantasizing about kissing her? That he'd been dreaming of stripping her naked and loving her until dawn? Wouldn't that make her day?

"Thinking about Jonathan Devlin and who would have wanted him dead."

"I'd like to talk to Gavin about the investigation."

"So would a lot of other reporters."

"Still, I'm going to call him when I'm in town tomorrow."

Logan shrugged. "It's worth a try," he agreed.

At the ranch, Melissa spent the afternoon compiling her notes and verifying her facts. While the stories about the anniversary of Royal and the vandalism of the Halifax exhibit were interesting, she decided she would use those stories to draw attention to the town's history and the legend of Jessamine Golden.

Having the map displayed while she did her report remained her goal. Maybe she'd been foolish to give in to Logan's ultimatum, but she knew she'd have to face him at some point and discuss their past. He wasn't going to let up until she did. At least now she'd get something she needed while satisfying his need to hash out what had happened between them.

Actually, Melissa was ready to get it over with. Thinking about whether or not she'd made a mistake years ago was exhausting. What if Cara Young had been wrong? What if Logan hadn't tried to use her?

No, he had. Logan's marriage shortly after she'd left was all the proof she needed.

Trying to get her mind off of Logan, she called Daniel to discuss the story. Melissa told him about Jonathan Devlin's murder and the possibility that it was tied to Jessamine Golden's map. She wasn't at all surprised when Daniel instructed her to keep digging to find a clear connection.

After hanging up with Daniel, she went to Rick's cottage. They spent an hour or so discussing their itinerary for the next day and talking about the map at the museum.

Heading back to the house, Melissa wondered if Logan had made the necessary arrangements for them to film the map. But she wasn't able to ask him because it wasn't until dinnertime that she saw him again.

When Melissa walked into the dining room, Logan looked up. "Hi, I'm sorry I kept you," she said.

"You didn't," he assured her. "Where's Rick?"

She chuckled. "He said he was going to a bar to check out the hot cowgirls. His description, not mine," she clarified. Logan was sitting at the end of the table so she took the seat to his right.

Melissa took one look at the starchy foods gracing the table along with the roast beef and green beans—macaroni and cheese and homemade biscuits—and nearly sighed. She loved this kind of meal, but usually kept herself on a more moderate diet. She took a helping of each and decided to enjoy the meal. Buttering a biscuit, she took a bite of it.

"This food is delicious. You know, I usually jog a few days a week at home to combat my indulgences. I should have bought some running shoes while I was in town. Maybe I will tomorrow."

"Speaking of tomorrow, what are your plans?"

She sipped her sweetened iced tea. "Rick and I are going to the museum. If all goes well, we may shoot a segment." She was dying to know about the map. Unable to wait for him to bring it up, she put her fork down and looked at him. "Did you find out if I can use the map in my story?"

"Yeah, it won't be a problem. Mark Hartman will keep an eye on it while you're using it."

She frowned. "Won't you be there to do that?" He'd said he was going everywhere she went. Apparently he hadn't meant it. She should have been pleased by the change in his plans, but couldn't deny feeling a bit disappointed.

Logan finished the last of his meal. "I'll be there."

Looking confused, she asked, "Then why won't you be guarding the map?"

He gave her a direct look. "Because I'll be watching you."

Melissa tilted her head as she thought about his answer. "Me? What on earth for?"

"Because if someone's after the map and you're using it, that makes you a target."

"I don't live in Royal. Why would anyone hurt me?"

He shrugged. "They might not want to hurt you, but if you get in their way, you could be in danger. The map will be out in the open near you so that's reason enough."

"I think you're worrying about nothing."

"Then it shouldn't bother you if I'm there to guard you."

"All right," she conceded. "But you're just wasting your time."

Logan seriously doubted that. Watching her could become his favorite pastime. Definitely a bedroom activity. "Now that you have approval to use the map, it's time you held up your end of the bargain."

Melissa finished the last bite of her meal and wiped her fingers clean with her napkin. "All right. But is there somewhere more comfortable we can talk?"

Logan stood. "We can go into my study."

Getting out of her seat, she preceded him into the hallway. She'd made a deal with him and he'd held up his end of the bargain. Now it was time for her to do the same. Well, that was fine by her. She couldn't wait to hear Logan admit the truth. After they talked, he would regret that he had forced the issue.

Stepping into his study, she looked around. When she'd been in here last night, she hadn't paid attention to the decor. Bookcases lined the wall behind a large wood desk where a computer sat. The brown sofa looked soft and inviting, as did the man-size chair in front of the desk. The faint scent of leather gave the room a masculine appeal.

"Make yourself comfortable," Logan said from behind her as he shut the door.

How was she supposed to do that? Except for the one on the day when she'd broken up with Logan, this was going to be the most difficult conversation she'd ever had.

Choosing one end of the sofa, she sat, then watched Logan move across the room to occupy the other end of it. He leaned toward her, his elbows resting on his knees, his hands clasped together.

Under his direct stare, doubts about her sanity in agreeing to talk with him arose. "I don't know exactly what you want to hear."

"Don't play coy, Melissa. You're too good at what you do to pull that off." She'd done good job of dodging his questions until now.

Her defenses went up. "You were good, too, Logan. Good at fooling me, making me believe you cared about me."

He frowned. "I loved you, Melissa. I thought you loved me until you broke up with me and said you were leaving to become a reporter."

Shaking her head, she said, "That's not why I left and you know it." Melissa had to give it to Logan. He still was trying to pretend that he was innocent of hurting her. Why? What good would it do him? He was the one who wanted to get to the truth.

"What are you talking about?"

She gave a bitter laugh. "You were using me and you know it."

"Using you?" He straightened. Suddenly he had a bad feeling about where this was going.

"I knew about your father's will."

Logan didn't move. How could she have known about his father's will? "What about it?" he asked carefully, panic thrumming through his pulse.

"You wanted to get this all out in the open," she stated harshly. "Tell me about how you asked me to marry you so you could hold on to all of this." She swept the room with her hand.

He felt the blood drain from his face. "I asked you to marry me because I was in love with you."

"Right. And the fact that if you married before your brother the ranch would be yours never played into it?"

He wanted to deny her accusation. Would she believe him if he did? Trying to figure out the best way to explain, he shifted topics to buy some time. "How did you know about the will?"

"So it was true." She didn't want to break down in front of him, didn't want him to know that what he'd done still mattered to her. But it did.

Logan couldn't lie to her. "That I'd get the ranch if I married before Bart did? Yes. But what did that have to do with us?"

Melissa dragged in a breath. Until now, she'd held out the tiniest hope she'd been wrong. Her chest ached at his betrayal. "Everything, Logan. I ran into a friend who had been dating Bart. Right before they stopped seeing each other, he'd told her everything, that you even bragged about beating him to the altar."

"That's not true, Melissa. Bart and I thought it worked out great, you and I getting married. I never bragged about anything to him."

"Really?" she said with sarcasm. "Tell me it's not true that you ask me to marry you to keep the ranch."

"I'll admit that learning about the stipulation changed my thinking, but only about the timetable of our relationship. I wouldn't have asked you to marry me if I hadn't loved you."

"Oh, Logan, I'm not that young, naive girl anymore."

"It's the truth," he persisted, hurt that she doubted him now as well as then. "You left me because you thought I'd marry you to keep the ranch?"

"You said as much to me the night you proposed," she reminded him.

Confused, he shook his head. "What did I say?"

"You said, 'I'll have everything I ever wanted, you and the Wild Spur.' I didn't know what you meant until I heard about the will."

Logan reached out to touch her, then stopped himself when he realized she didn't seem receptive to his gesture. "I don't even remember saying that, Melissa. I just know that I loved you. I did. It was hell when you left me."

Had she misinterpreted the meaning of his words? Melissa wanted to believe him, but her distrust was hard to overcome.

"You loved me so much that you married another woman?" she challenged.

Logan's breath exploded in his lungs. "You know about Cara?" Hell, this was getting worse.

Her eyes speared his. "Cara?" For a moment she couldn't speak as she processed his words, then her heart sank with their meaning. "Cara Young?" When he nodded, she hunched forward and placed her hands over her face, dragging in deep breaths, wishing she was anywhere but there. Why had he been so adamant about dredging up the past when the result was that she'd be hurt even more?

"Melissa?"

Suddenly he felt like scum. Logan had never felt more helpless than at that moment. He wanted to hold her, comfort her, but he held himself back.

Melissa lifted her face and looked at him, her cheeks flushed. "You married Cara Young?"

"Yes, but—"

"Damn you." Her eyes glittered with tears as she stood. "Were you seeing her while we were dating?"

"No!" Logan said. "I swear I wasn't. I didn't even meet her until after you left."

"How could you not have known her? She was dating your brother."

Logan's expression changed to confusion. "She never dated Bart. He knew her, sure. He was the one who introduced us. After a few months of seeing each other, she kept saying that she loved me, that she wanted to get married." He shrugged. "So…we did."

"Let me get this straight, Logan. You loved me. But

after I left, you met Cara, and after a few months when she kept saying how much she loved you, you married her?"

"It sounds bad, I know. I was miserable after you left. On the rebound from you, I married her. It was a stupid thing to do. Our marriage lasted less than a year. I'm sure that she never dated Bart. They were just friends."

Melissa shook her head, confused. Something wasn't right here. "Logan, she dated Bart."

"That's not possible."

"Apparently it was." She released a slow breath. "It was Cara Young who told me about your father's will."

Seven

Logan's eyes glittered with anger. "What?"

"Cara dated Bart. They'd been seeing each other for a while before they broke up."

"That can't be true," he said, his words hot with denial. He had no idea where she'd heard such a thing, but she was mistaken.

"The day I ran into her, Bart had already told her about the will and had broken up with her," Melissa said, her throat dry. "Cara had been so angry at your brother. She said she'd wanted to marry Bart so he'd get the ranch. Then they could sell it and live off the money. But Bart had said he wasn't interested in getting married and he was leaving town as soon as he got his money."

"It's true that Bart wanted only the money, not the ranch." Logan cursed beneath his breath. Everything was beginning to make sense. "If what you're saying is true, she must have told you about the will to get back at Bart. If we broke up, he wouldn't have gotten anything."

Melissa swallowed hard. "I'm telling you the truth, Logan. Cara was really upset that day. She wanted to marry Bart."

"Did she? From the way she came on to me, it seems like she wanted the money even more," he answered soberly. He felt like a fool. Cara had used him.

"Maybe she did. But that doesn't explain why your own brother would have set you up by introducing her to you."

"Yes, it does," he said, aching at the cold actions of his brother. "That's how much he wanted to leave Royal. The only way for him to get the money was to get married, or to make sure I did."

Rising, he paced the room. "When you and I were engaged, he must have figured it wouldn't be long before he got his cash. Knowing he'd be leaving and with Cara pressuring him to propose, he must have ended things with her." Logan should have seen through Cara, but during that time, he'd been blinded by the pain of Melissa leaving.

Melissa looked at Logan. "And when I broke up with you, it messed up Bart's plans."

"Yeah." He gave a bitter laugh. "He wanted his money bad enough to conspire with his ex-girlfriend to get it." Bart always had been selfish, and after he'd left Royal, they rarely had seen each other. As brothers they'd never been close, had never been friends. Now, they never would be.

She stood and walked over to him. "How could he have done that?"

"After my mother died, my father doted on Bart, gave him anything he wanted. Bart was used to having his way. I guess he figured that applied to the money as well."

She touched his arm. "They why didn't your father just leave the ranch to Bart? Why put the stipulation in the will about one of you getting married?"

"Honestly, I'm not sure," Logan answered, baffled. "My father was a difficult man to understand. He didn't talk much, kept a lot inside. I think he knew how much I wanted the ranch, but he loved Bart more. Maybe my father thought it would make Brad grow up and settle down."

"Oh, Logan, I'm so sorry," Melissa said on a soft whisper. Despite what had happened between them, how much it had stung when she'd found out Logan had married another woman, she felt deep sorrow for him. It must have been hard being raised in the shadow of his brother.

"I'm the one who's sorry. Bart ruined what we had together." God, he couldn't believe it. All these years he'd blamed Melissa. Bart had stolen their past together. Anger boiled inside him. If he ever saw his brother again, there wouldn't be enough left of him to think about.

"And Cara Young." She turned toward him. "Leaving you broke my heart. I loved you so much then."

"So you didn't leave for a career?" he asked, his eyes questioning.

She bit her lip, then a moment later said, "No. I just said that to save face. I didn't want you to know how much you'd hurt me."

"I hope you can believe now that I loved you, too."

She shrugged. "I want to." It wasn't easy to give him her trust. Or to let the past go. But the attraction between them…oh, that was something else altogether.

Logan draped his arm around her and pulled her close to him. Giving in to the need to be held by him, she rested her head against his chest with a sigh.

"But you're not sure?" He understood. No matter what she said, it still hurt him that she'd left him.

Looking up at him, she said, "It's hard to believe that you married Cara."

He swallowed past the knot in his throat. "I made a terrible mistake."

"I don't think what happened between us is something we can easily get past. But I want you know one thing." Her heart pounded wildly inside her. "I'm still attracted to you," she said candidly. "Does that count for anything?"

He sighed and the tension left his body. "Oh, yeah, sweetheart. I'm attracted to you, too."

"Let's enjoy what time we have now, Logan." She wasn't staying. They led different lives in different cities. More importantly, she refused to lead her heart into such danger again. But she wanted this moment with him, wanted a chance to rediscover what they'd had together, to learn about the man he'd become.

Though she hadn't said the words, Logan knew what she meant. "I like the way you think," he whispered huskily, then covered her mouth with his.

Melissa sank into his kiss. The feelings she'd kept locked inside were threatening to break loose. Could she stop them? Did she have a choice? Despite the promise she'd made to herself before she came back, she wanted to be with Logan again. Could she indulge in an affair with him and leave with her heart intact?

If she couldn't, was she ready to face the consequences of sleeping with him, then walking away again?

He groaned as she kissed him back and pressed his erection against her. "You always did have that power over me," he whispered. He cupped her breast with his hand, massaged it gently.

Melissa's knees went weak. She licked her lips, tasting him, wanting more than ever to feel his powerful body inside hers.

Logan ran his tongue along her lips, then past her teeth to explore her mouth. Heat exploded through him. Sweet. Tender. Exotic. She sucked on his tongue and he moved his hips in response.

"Should we be doing this here?" she asked quietly when he shifted his attention to her throat. Even as she'd asked the question, her mouth sought his in a heady, explosive kiss that left them both breathing hard.

Logan continued to touch his lips to hers with a nibbling, seductive motion that teased and tempted. "Want to go to my room?"

"Yes," she answered in a desperate sigh. Gliding her hands around his neck, she dragged his mouth down to hers. He nipped her lips with his teeth.

"I've never forgotten your taste," he told her huskily. "Never." He'd tried. Hell, all these years he'd been haunted by it. But Melissa was in his soul. There was a connection between them that separation hadn't erased. "After all this time, I want you in my bed."

All night. And he suspected making love to her all night long wouldn't be enough to atone for years of wanting her.

She took his hand in hers and he led the way through the house to the room across the hall from her own. Once inside, she glanced around. His bedroom was large and masculine, decorated in burgundy and brown with an inviting king-size bed. "This is nice," she said. With a sexy smile, she added, "I really like the bed."

Logan's eyes flashed with desire. "Then come share it with me." He drew her to it, sat and pulled her toward him. She stood before him, her hands on his shoulders as he began unfastening the buttons of her blouse. It fell in a heap to the floor.

Melissa leaned down and kissed him as his hands covered her breasts, moaning softly as he caressed them through her bra. She unfastened his shirt and pushed it off him, then explored his hard-muscled shoulders, his corded neck.

It had been a long time since she'd been with him, but suddenly it felt as though it was only yesterday. There was no pretense, no awkwardness, no hesitancy to give herself to him. Her body was attuned to his and he was an expert at igniting her passion. Continuing to kiss her, he found the catch of her bra. With little effort he released it and she freed her arms. His tongue continued doing wonderful things to her mouth as his hands again found her breasts, his fingers pleasuring her.

"Logan." She held her breath as his mouth moved lower, pressing hot kisses to her throat, her shoulder. Lower and lower until his hot mouth closed over her tight, rigid nipple. A fever began simmering deep inside her as she moaned. Her hands held his neck, pressing him to her.

"You are so beautiful," Logan murmured, then he divided his attention between her nipples, kissing one then the other, laving them with his tongue.

His words, whispered in passion, fueled her desire. "I want you," she told him. Her body was no longer hers. It belonged to him and only he knew how to soothe the delicious ache building inside her.

Lifting his head, he leveled his gaze on her. "I've wanted you ever since I saw you at the ball," he confessed. He lay back on the bed, taking her with him, then he rolled her to her back and stretched out beside her. He unfastened her slacks and skimmed his hand along her warm, velvet skin. His fingers grazed the tuft of hair between her legs. Cupping her, he slipped them between the yielding folds.

Hot. Soft. Wet.

For him.

"You're driving me wild," she whispered. "Come inside me." The words were boldly spoken, a challenge that let him know she was ready for him.

"Woman, you really know how to turn me on."

Her gaze drifted over him, pausing on the bulge in his jeans. Her eyes met his again. "Show me."

Logan left the bed. He hooked his fingers in the waistband of her pants and drew them down over her thighs, removing them along with her heels. As he shed his jeans, he made love to her mouth. She rewarded him with a groan of satisfaction and longing. Her hips rocked back and forth as he caressed between her legs, stroking her slowly, making her ready for him.

It took every ounce of strength for Logan to stop touching her, but he moved his hand up her body to her breast, then whispered, "I'll be right back."

Melissa dragged her eyes open. "Where are you going?"

"I need to protect you."

"Right."

He opened the drawer to the nightstand beside his bed, then returned with a foil packet in his hand. His gaze locked with hers, he stood before her, naked. All of him. All six-foot-three of rugged, muscled man.

All hers.

At least for the moment.

She banished that thought from her mind as he sheathed himself. Melissa's throat went dry, her desire for him intensifying as he moved over her and spread her legs apart, positioning himself.

Wanting to enjoy every single moment of loving Melissa, Logan took it slow, joining their bodies, then withdrawing. Inch by aching inch he filled her, her body stretching to accommodate him. She opened her legs wider, and as he pushed himself fully inside her, he kissed her again and again, building their ecstasy, bringing her to the brink of the ultimate pleasure. Her hips began writhing against his own, and still he made love to her in slow, rhythmic strokes.

"Oh, Logan." Melissa whispered his name, half plea, half demand. He seemed to know intuitively what she wanted, moving faster, plunging deeper into her over and over. Her arms went around him, holding him to her, wanting the rush of heat to last forever.

But it didn't and her release came swiftly. She closed her eyes and gave herself to him completely. Shifting against him, she chased the gratification he promised with each movement of his body inside hers. And then she was falling over the edge of bliss as sensations exploded through her.

She tightened her arms as he pushed even deeper, seeking his own release. When it came, he groaned and his hands gripped her, claiming her as his.

After a few moments, when she could breathe again, Melissa ran her hand along Logan's back. His body was hard, lean, his skin so hot. It felt wonderfully delicious to have the freedom to touch him so intimately.

Logan shifted his weight from Melissa, then held her as he tried to catch his breath. She sighed and moved closer to him, ran her hand along his belly. His muscles clenched at her touch. He'd gone into this with his eyes wide open. He had told himself that he could handle his attraction to her, that he could handle what was happening between them, and come out unscathed.

Now he wasn't so sure—one taste of her and he wanted more.

He forced himself to face facts. Melissa had walked away from him before and she was going to again, this time for another reason. The difference now was that he knew it.

His pulse began to slow and he couldn't stop himself from asking, "Why didn't you talk to me, Melissa?" He had to know in order to put what had happened totally behind him.

She raised her eyelids and looked at him, regretting that she hadn't given him the benefit of the doubt. "I thought I knew the truth after what Cara had said. It pretty much confirmed what you'd said the night you proposed. I was hurt. I was so young, Logan, and you were so…" she smiled "…so male. You knew exactly what you wanted. It was a little overwhelming for me. I should have talked to you. I know that now." She gave a soft shrug. Realizing she'd played a part in their breakup staggered her.

Cara. His gut twisted. How could he wonder why Melissa had listened to Cara's lies? Like a fool, he'd trusted Cara, too. And his brother. "Hell, sweetheart, we both believed her."

She ran her hand along his shoulder, then touched his face. "I thought if you loved me, you'd come after me."

"I did love you." Logan raised himself above her.

She stared into his eyes. "Why didn't you try to find me?"

He swallowed hard. "At first I thought you wanted a career as a reporter and I didn't want to stand in your way."

"At first?"

"I've never been good at this kind of thing, Melissa," he confessed.

She frowned. "What kind of thing?"

"Talking. Sharing what I'm thinking. My mother was gone early in my life and my father wasn't very sociable. Bart and I never got along. I never had anyone to talk to. After some time had passed, it was easier for me to let you go than to deal with why you left."

Melissa reached up and kissed his cheek. "You're getting better at it," she said. "Logan, why didn't you tell me about the will?" she asked, needing to know.

"God, sweetheart, I don't know. I guess somewhere inside I was afraid you'd think exactly what you did, that I was using you."

Which showed he hadn't trusted her feelings for him, Melissa thought. No more than she'd trusted what he felt for her. "I guess we were both young and vulnerable." Now, though together temporarily, they'd both changed.

Except her love for him hadn't faded at all. It was still there, threatening to consume her.

Logan traced her thigh with his finger, running up her rib cage to her nipple. He began toying with it and she sighed sweetly. Aroused, he moved over her, straddling her thighs. Her auburn hair spread out on his pillow and he couldn't get enough of looking at her.

Melissa felt his hardness pressing against her as his mouth took hers on a passionate journey.

Sweet.

Sensitive.

Hot.

Demanding.

Her eyes closed as she arched against him and eagerly responded to his lovemaking. He shifted and his hands found hers. Holding them on both sides of her head, he pushed inside her when she opened her legs for him.

Logan groaned as he ground his hips against hers. "Open your eyes, Melissa. I want to see you come apart for me."

She did and met his burning gaze. His eyes held hers

in a spell as he pushed even more intimately into her. The sensual journey began again, slowly at first, then building in intensity until she could no longer think. Her mind splintered in a thousand pieces as he ground his teeth together and called out her name, taking them both over the cliff of ecstasy.

Within that precious moment, Melissa knew Logan had broken through the barriers she'd erected around her heart.

Melissa stirred and lazily opened her eyes. Morning sunshine peeked through the curtains. She lay in bed with Logan, her body pressed against his. It had been a long time since she'd spent the night with a man, but with Logan it felt so natural.

Their night together had been incredible. Logan had been tender, yet demanding, evoking a response from her that only he was capable of. Melissa had never forgotten how Logan's touch could build her desire for him until she couldn't do anything except feel how perfectly they responded to each other.

It had always been like that between them. And, oh, it was almost devastating to know it still was.

Until now she'd never faced the truth. Moving away from him hadn't purged her love for Logan from her heart. She'd only successfully kept it locked away where she wouldn't have to analyze her feelings.

So where did that leave her?

For the past several years, she'd focused on her career. She'd worked her butt off to move up the ladder of success. Now, this promotion was at her fingertips.

It was what she wanted, right?

She sighed wearily. For the first time, she wasn't sure. Being with Logan was incredible. There had been no feeling that she'd been making a mistake. Here, in his arms, was where she wanted to be.

"What's wrong?" Logan asked, his voice hoarse from sleep. He'd heard Melissa's sigh and alarms went off inside him. Was she regretting sleeping with him?

Melissa turned in his arms until she was facing him. "Nothing."

She smiled, but he saw sadness lingering in her eyes. He suspected she was holding something back, but, not willing to break their fragile bond, he didn't push her. "Are you all right?"

"Oh, yeah." She stretched, then trailed her hand down his chest to his flat stomach. "How about you?"

Logan's hips moved as blood surged through his body. His erection was immediate and intense. His gaze met hers. "Take your hand lower and you'll find out."

She did, and he groaned with pleasure as she stroked him. Leaning closer, she kissed him deeply as her hand continued to explore him. He was hard and smooth, and oh, so hot.

After a moment, Logan clamped his hand around her wrist. "If you don't stop, you're not going to be able to join the party."

"Well, we can't have that, can we?" She made quick work of the condom, then shifted over him, straddling him, taking him inside her.

Logan pushed deeply into her until he was completely surrounded by her feminine heat. "No, sweetheart, we can't." Straining, he held back his release as she began moving her hips. His hands cupped her breasts, massaged her nipples, then skimmed to her back and pulled her to him.

"You feel so good inside me," she murmured, her breathing growing rapid as gratification swiftly changed to an ache so desperate that she thought she'd die if he stopped moving. Her body convulsed as her climax began. "Now, Logan," she cried, and let him take over the rhythm.

Logan's hips rocked faster, until she tightened all around him and cried out his name. His own climax came and, unable to hold back, he joined her in the sweet release, his pleasure deep and intense, overwhelming him. And he knew Melissa had not only eased his desire for her.

She'd eased the ache in his heart.

Eight

Breathing heavily, Melissa lay sprawled across Logan. "I hope you have a drawer full of those." She raised herself up and gave him a teasing look.

Logan grinned at her. "Don't worry. If we run out and you get pregnant, I'll make an honest woman of you."

Although he was joking, his words touched a place in her heart. If she hadn't been so naive ten years ago, she'd already be his wife and maybe they'd have had children. But that could never happen now. "Right. And you'd move to Houston?" She shook her head. "I don't think so."

He propped his arm on the bed and watched her gather her clothes. A tense silence fell between them. Melissa stopped in the process of looking for her bra and faced him. "C'mon, Logan, let's not fool ourselves.

What's happened between us is wonderful, but it can't last. We both know it."

Logan sobered. She'd said the words he'd been thinking ever since they'd kissed last night. He'd told himself that he could live for the moment, that he could be happy being with Melissa—making love to her—even if it couldn't last between them. Hearing her confirm his own thoughts disturbed him more than he'd expected. "Yeah, I know." But he didn't have to like it.

She licked her lips. "I don't want any secrets between us, Logan." She sat on the edge of the bed, leaned over and kissed him, sighing when his tongue met hers. She ended their kiss and looked at him, unsure what to think of the apprehension in his eyes.

"Can you stay for a while after your story is done?"

She shook her head. "I'm up for a promotion as soon as I return."

He raised his eyebrows. "What kind of promotion?"

"There's an opening for a weekend news anchor. If everything falls into place, this should be my last assignment as a reporter."

A dull pain stabbed him in the chest at the thought of her leaving. As much as he wanted her to stay, he didn't have the right to ask her to. She'd worked hard to get where she was. It would be selfish to ask her to give it up. "I see."

At his quick compliance, sadness filled her. What had she wanted? That he'd beg her to stay? If she were honest, a part of her had. Which was a foolish thought. Her life was in Houston. "It's what I do, Logan."

"I know." She was being forthright with him, and he

had to accept it or risk ruining what time they had left together.

Melissa brushed her fingertips across his forehead. "I've got to get dressed. If I don't find Rick, he's liable to go off on some cowboy roundup or something. I think he's forgotten that he's working."

Logan drew her to him for a kiss, then let her go. She stood and looked down at him. "Do you have a robe or something? I don't want to get caught sneaking across the hall-naked."

"Hold on."

Logan went into the bathroom and returned with a blue terry robe. Its thick softness enfolded her as he helped her into it. Breathing deeply, she noticed his scent clung to it. She halfway decided to take it when she left. "Thanks."

"You're welcome." He hugged her. "When are you going into town?"

"Within the hour. I'm going to ask Sheriff O'Neal if he'll release the pictures of the Halifax Exhibit vandalism. Then Rick and I will scope out the museum and determine if I've chosen the best place to tape. We'll visit the library, too. They probably have a genealogy section, which will have a lot of facts."

"I'll come with you."

Melissa recognized his no-nonsense tone, remembered his intent to shadow her. But that had been before they'd slept together and she'd believed his motives were to talk about their past. "Logan, you don't have to babysit me."

Logan pulled on his jeans. Although she wasn't concerned about danger, he wanted to be with her. With Jonathan Devlin's murder under investigation, Logan didn't feel comfortable with Melissa asking questions around town on her own. He didn't care if it was her job or not. He wanted her safe while she was here, while he could take the liberty to watch over her. "I want a chance to see you work."

Surprised, she grinned. "We won't film today. We'll just go over some of the details," she told him, pleased he was interested in her work. "I'll meet you at breakfast in about an hour. I hope Rick will be there. If you see him first, tell him we're going into town."

Leaning up on her toes, she kissed his mouth. What started out as a simple kiss grew into an intimate mating of their tongues. With reluctance, she pulled away. "You're trying to sidetrack me."

Logan skimmed his hand down until he cupped her breast. "Is it working?"

"Yes, which is why I'm leaving now. Another minute and I'm going to have my way with you."

He groaned. "You're killing me."

When he reached for her again, she batted his hands away and walked to the door. "Work, then play."

"Is that a promise?"

Melissa looked back and gave him a wink. "No, honey, that's a threat." She darted out before he could answer.

Several days later, Melissa and Rick began preparations for filming from the Historical Society Museum. She'd spent the past few days researching Jessamine

Golden and had gleaned a wealth of material at the local library with the help of the informative staff. Gavin O'Neal had granted her a few minutes of his time, as well as photos of the Halifax Exhibit vandalism. In the meantime Jonathan Devlin's autopsy results had reached the Devlin family and Logan had told her they were anxious for his killer to be caught.

She and Rick had nosed around town on their own. It seemed there was a lot of interest in Jessamine's map. Word had gotten out that Melissa would be filming today and a crowd had gathered to watch, more visitors than usual for the middle of the morning.

Aaron Hill, the director of the museum, had met with her yesterday, and he'd shared his knowledge of the intriguing Jessamine Golden legend. It was going to make quite an interesting story.

A nervous energy filled the room as Rick positioned the camera at the correct angle for shooting the segment. If there was indeed gold hidden somewhere in Royal, Melissa felt the map held the key. She looked around at the many people gathered to watch—Aaron, the museum employees and visitors—and couldn't help but wonder if one of them was Jonathan's murderer.

Logan stood at one of the entrances to the gallery, mesmerized by Melissa's movements as she talked with her videographer. Due to a special function being held at the museum, they hadn't been able to do the shoot the previous day, but the director had given them permission for today.

Dressed in a red blouse and a black suit with a skirt

that came to her knees, Melissa looked both beautiful and professional—the essence of a career news reporter focused on her responsibilities as she prepared for filming. Logan had been here for a couple of hours, keeping an eye on things as Melissa and Rick worked. Now Rick was doing the last sound check as Melissa went over her notes again.

It almost hurt to watch her. This was what she lived for.

Hearing his name called, he turned to see Mark Hartman walking toward him. "Hey, Mark."

"Logan." Mark scanned the area. "What do you want me to do?"

"Melissa is about ready to film. With so many extra visitors here today, Aaron asked that we be more vigilant when the map is out of the display case. Stand at that entrance and keep your eyes on the map at all times. It's going to be on that podium." He pointed to the stand in the center of the room. "My focus is going to be on Melissa as well as the map."

Understanding flashed in Mark's eyes. "You're involved with her."

Logan gave his friend a dark look. "We knew each other a long time ago." He didn't confirm or deny Mark's comment.

"The way you disappeared from the ball together, I figured that." Mark adjusted his hat, then his gaze traveled to Melissa and back.

Color climbed into Logan's face. "I hadn't expected to see her there," he answered. "We had a few things to discuss in private." The rest of his friends had yet to mention it, but he suspected the time was coming when they would.

"You were in love with her once?"

Swallowing hard, Logan nodded. "Yeah."

"And now?"

Logan shrugged. "Now we lead separate lives. Hers is in Houston."

"And she's going back?" Mark asked, his tone subdued.

"Yes. When she's finished with her work here."

He frowned. "Do you think she's in danger?"

"I don't know, but with Jonathan's murder, we can't rule out that someone may be desperate enough to kill to get the map." Logan looked around. The visitors were gathering to watch. Surrounded by glass walls, the gallery was accessible from two doorways. Logan was standing at one. "I'm not taking any chances with Melissa's life. I'll be watching from this angle." He pointed across the room to the door opposite him. "With you over there, we'll have a good view of everything."

"Right."

Melissa walked up to them, and Logan broke off the conversation to put his arm around her possessively. "Melissa, this is a friend of mine, Mark Hartman."

Melissa smiled at Logan's handsome friend. Nearly as tall as Logan, his cropped black hair and teakwood brown skin set off his hazel eyes. "It's nice to meet you, Mr. Hartman."

"My pleasure, Miss Mason," Mark returned, his slow Texas drawl seeming to caress his words. "Please, call me Mark."

"All right, if you'll call me Melissa. I appreciate your helping us out today, Mark. I hope this won't take long. One take, maybe two, and we should have it."

Rick signaled to her.

"I think we're about ready."

"Take your time. If you'll excuse me, I'm going to take up residence at the back of the room." Mark sauntered away.

Meeting Melissa's eyes, Logan pulled her closer. "I'd kiss you, but I don't want to wreck your makeup."

She laughed, then lifted her face. "Don't let that stop you. My lipstick is right here in my pocket." She patted her hip.

Logan gave in to his need to taste her, albeit briefly. His mouth touched hers, lingered momentarily, then he set her away from him. "You'd better go before I get carried away."

Her gaze glittered with awareness. "See you in a few minutes."

Logan watched her walk to the middle of the room. She picked up the microphone and waited for her cue. After a few moments, Rick gave her a prompt, then she began speaking. Pride filled him. Melissa was articulate and savvy, her voice eloquent and expressive. It was easy to understand why she'd been offered the anchor position.

A pang struck his heart as Logan thought of her returning to Houston. But he steeled himself to accept that she wasn't his to have.

Not all those years ago.

Not today.

Logan heard a loud *crack* and his body tensed as he scanned the room, unsure of what had caused the sound.

Another crack reverberated, this time louder and more threatening.

Logan's gaze shot to the iron chandelier above Melissa. It was shaking precariously. At the juncture of its base, plaster crumbled as the chandelier began to rip away from the ceiling.

"Logan!" Mark shouted from across the room at that same instant.

Logan bolted for Melissa as people began screaming. In one fluid motion, he tackled her, protecting her from the fall with his body as they hit the floor. Holding her tight, he rolled away from where she'd been standing a second before.

Iron landed with a thud as glass shattered, spilling across the floor like fragmented diamonds. Logan felt a sting as a piece of flying glass hit his forehead.

As the chandelier settled, screams from the fleeing observers filled the sudden stillness. He steadied himself, looking around to see if he could spot any further danger. Still covering Melissa, he saw Mark racing toward them and waved him off. "Secure the museum!" he shouted, then he lifted himself off Melissa.

"Are you all right?" Not waiting for her to answer, he ran his hands over her, checking for himself. She'd almost been killed. Fury rushed through him as he wrapped his arms around her.

Melissa sat up and touched her head. "I'm a little bruised, but I think so." Her heart pounded as she realized what had happened.

At risk to his own life, Logan had saved hers! A few more seconds and the chandelier would have crushed her. Her knees shook as he helped her stand. Then she saw the cut on his forehead. "You're bleeding! Oh, my

God." A streak of red oozed from his wound and began to trickle into his dark eyebrow.

"I'm all right," Logan insisted, though he felt the warm dampness on his skin. Reaching up, he brushed at it with his fingers, then wiped his hand on his jeans.

"No, you're not." She pressed her hand against his head to try to stop the flow.

He put his hand over hers. "I'm fine. It's just a scratch," he assured her.

Worried, she lifted her hand so she could look at it. "It needs tending."

His heart warmed at her concerned expression. "I'll let you take care of it personally once we sort this out."

Melissa sighed as she pulled her hand away. Though his wound continued to ooze, it didn't appear to be a deep cut. "All right," she answered, not happy about waiting. They shook the remaining shards of glass from their clothing. Looking around the room, she searched for her videographer. "Rick!"

"Yeah?" Rick shouted over the din.

"Are you okay?"

He nodded as he rubbed his shoulder.

"See if you can get some of this," she said. "We can use the footage with our story."

Rick lifted the camera to his shoulder and began scanning the room.

"You don't miss a beat," Logan commented.

"It's my job," she answered simply. "What on earth happened?" She stared aghast at the clutter around them. The broken chandelier lay crookedly on top of the podium, which was turned over and partially broken. Glass and shards of wood littered the black marble floor, which had cracked from the impact.

"You were nearly killed, that's what."

The implication of how close she'd come to dying hit her again as Aaron Hill rushed up to them. "Miss Mason, are you all right?"

"I think so."

"I'm so sorry. I don't know how this happened," he exclaimed, his face red. "What can I do for you?"

"Please, see to your employees and visitors," Melissa suggested.

"And don't let anyone leave," Logan ordered.

"Of course."

They watched him hurry away and disappear into the crowd of people outside the room. "I can't believe this." Melissa looked around. "How could the chandelier fall?"

"I don't know." At this point, Logan suspected it wasn't an accident, so he wasn't letting Melissa out of his sight until he knew her life wasn't in danger.

Her gaze took in the hole in the ceiling, swept the room, then landed on the toppled podium.

The map!

A sick feeling came over her as she pulled away from Logan. Her pulse began to accelerate again and a knot formed in her throat. "Oh, no."

Please don't let it be gone!

One glance at her and Logan knew something was wrong. "What is it?"

"I don't see the map." Carefully navigating her way,

Melissa went to the podium, broken glass crunching beneath her steps. Logan was hot on her heels.

Together they searched the area. The map wasn't anywhere to be seen.

"Damn." Logan let out a harsh breath. Someone *had* been after the map. Melissa's use of it had provided the perfect opportunity. Her life had meant nothing to whoever wanted it.

Dread filled Melissa's stomach. It had been at her request that the map had been unsecured. "I'm so sorry, Logan."

"It's not your fault." Rage tore through him as he looked at the chandelier again, and he thought about what it could have done to her.

"Yes, it is. The map was out because of my story. You warned me about the possibility of danger, but I didn't take you seriously."

"If someone killed Jonathan Devlin because they were after the map, they could have gotten their hands on it by breaking into the museum. Filming your story only gave them another option."

She caught her breath at the anger on his face. "I've put you in a bad position. I don't know what to say."

He stared at her. "You think I'm angry at you?" She bit her lip and nodded. "God, no. But whoever did this is going to be sorry when I get my hands on them." He stroked her hair from her face.

Mark walked up, tucking his cell phone in his pocket. "I've called Gavin. He's on the way."

"The map is missing," Logan informed his friend.

"What?" Mark took in the damage to the podium.

"Damn." His jaw muscle twitched as a look of guilt filled his face. "I took my eyes off it after everything broke loose. Like you, I was heading for Melissa." He swore a few choice words under his breath, then looked at Melissa. "Sorry."

"That's okay, Mark. I'm the one who's responsible. This wouldn't have happened if I hadn't asked for the map to be displayed," she told him.

"Let's focus on getting it back," Logan suggested.

"The camera!" Melissa said suddenly. "Maybe we caught the thief on film." She glanced around for Rick. Spotting him across the room, she walked over to him, Logan and Mark right behind her.

Rick stopped filming and looked at them. "Yeah?"

"We need your help." She introduced Mark to her coworker, then explained that during the commotion, Jessamine Golden's map had been stolen. "We're hoping you caught the thief on film. When did you stop shooting?"

He shook his head. "I didn't. The camera's been running the whole time. I heard someone shout, then I heard a loud *crack*. The next thing I knew someone knocked into me. I almost dropped the camera."

"I'm sorry about that," Logan apologized, knowing he was the one who'd crashed into Rick. "I only had seconds to get to Melissa."

"It's okay," Rick said, rolling his shoulder as if to check for pain.

"Can you run the film back and play it for us?" Melissa asked.

"Sure." Rick pushed the buttons on the camera, reset the film, then put it on play mode and turned the small screen toward them. The replay showed Melissa speaking, then began to blur. "This is when Logan pushed me," he told them.

Logan muttered an oath when the screen showed distorted footage for the next minute, then it returned to normal. Rick rewound it and played it again for them.

"Stop it there." Logan pointed to a blurred image moving into range in the direction of the podium. "That's our thief."

"It's not much help," Mark commented. "You can't even tell if it's a man or a woman."

"Maybe you could if I put it on a video and you played it on a bigger screen," Rick suggested.

Logan's gaze cut to him. "Good idea. Can you do that for us?"

"Sure, but I'll need access to some equipment."

"Would they have the equipment you need at a television station here in Royal?" Mark asked. He and Logan shared a look.

Rick shrugged his shoulders. "Probably. I think we have an affiliate station here in Royal, WRYL. It'll take a few phone calls, but I can probably use their equipment once I get permission."

"Don't worry about it. We'll arrange it," Logan told him.

Rick raised his eyebrows. "You can do that?"

Mark reached for his cell phone. "Consider it done," he said, then he left them.

"All right," Rick said. "Let me know when I can go there. Until we leave, I'm going to shoot some more footage," he told Melissa.

Melissa waited until Rick had walked away. "Let me get this straight. One phone call and we have access to a room full of technical equipment at a local television station?"

Logan studied her curious expression. "We have contacts."

"Sheesh." She blew out a breath. "Who else do you have contact with? The President?" she asked flippantly.

Grinning, Logan admitted, "We've chatted a time or two."

Nine

Three hours later, Melissa and Logan were still at the museum. The area where the accident had occurred had been cordoned off with yellow crime scene tape. Sheriff O'Neal had arrived on the scene quickly and Logan had left Melissa to talk with him. A short while later he'd returned and informed her the sheriff wanted her to wait until he'd cleared the museum of everyone else.

Logan and Mark had assisted the sheriff by talking with witnesses and taking notes until everyone had been interviewed. Melissa watched them work, impressed by their efficient handling of the crisis. She was seated on a folding chair that a museum employee had gotten for her when Logan and Sheriff O'Neal finally approached her. She stood and held out her hand in greeting. A handsome man, the sheriff's muscular body moved with authority and confidence.

"Melissa, I'm sorry to make you wait so long."

"I understand." She smiled, but inside her heart was beating harder and faster than normal. "Believe me, as a reporter I'm used it."

Gavin flicked a glance around them. "Only a tornado could have caused more damage. You have my word we'll do a thorough investigation. I'd like to hear what happened from you. Though we're lucky to have your video, it may not have been focused on something that will help us solve the case."

She shrugged. "I'll tell you what I can." She recounted how she'd been taping her story when the ceiling fixture fell.

"Did you hear anything suspicious?"

"I heard a loud noise, like something breaking or ripping. I'm not sure which. After that, I heard it again, louder." She looked up. The chandelier had left a jagged hole in the ceiling when it pulled free.

"Pretty much everyone else's story," Logan commented. "Including mine."

"Then what happened?" the sheriff asked.

She smiled at him. "Then I was hit by a two-hundred-pound man."

Gavin smothered a grin when his gaze met Logan's. "What happened next?"

"I was on the floor, Logan on top of me. I didn't realize the fixture had fallen until I got up and looked around. Logan rescued me just in time. Do you have any idea of how this could have happened?"

"From what we can tell right now, the bolts holding the chandelier came loose and it fell."

Though Gavin's expression remained composed, Melissa detected the underlying thread of anger in his tone. "So someone could have tampered with it?"

He shrugged. "It's one of the possibilities."

She gave him a direct look. "Which means it wasn't an accident?"

He nodded.

Melissa thought about that. "So whoever was responsible, were they targeting me or were they after the map?"

"At this point I'm not sure."

"Am I in danger?"

Shooting a look at Logan, Gavin raised his eyebrows. "Why do I feel like I'm the one being interviewed?"

Logan smiled wryly. "She's a reporter, remember?"

Melissa's instincts told her they were holding back information. "Something else is going on here. That the chandelier fell is strange enough, but then the map disappeared. This *accident* is tied into Jonathan Devlin's murder, isn't it?"

Folding his notebook, Gavin tucked it in his pocket. "That case is still under investigation. As to whether they're related, it's too soon to reach that conclusion. We're not ready to reveal any of our findings on Jonathan Devlin's murder to the press."

She gave his comment consideration, then said, "I can appreciate that, Sheriff, but I'm obligated to report to my station what I've learned."

He met her gaze. "Fair enough. How about if you

sit on this for a while and when it breaks, you get the exclusive?"

"All right," she agreed, knowing in the end she'd get an even bigger story—one that would further boost her career. A nice finish to her reporting days before her leap to a desk assignment. "I'll keep it quiet for now."

Gavin nodded. "Until we know more, be careful. Whoever did this could be trying to stop you from bringing attention to the map and alerting others that it could lead to a treasure. Even if it doesn't, the perpetrator may think it does and not want anyone to get in his way of finding it."

They said goodbye and after the hectic day, Melissa was more than ready to leave. By the time she and Logan arrived at the ranch, exhaustion had hit her. Her nerves were shot and her muscles were sore and stiff. It had been easy to function right after the accident while her adrenaline was pumping, but once the excitement was over, her energy had disappeared. She leaned against Logan as they walked to the house together.

Norah met them at the door. "What happened? Someone called and said there was an accident at the museum." She surveyed the two of them and noticed Melissa disheveled appearance and the cut on Logan's head.

"A chandelier fell near where Melissa was filming."

"My goodness! Are you all right?" she asked Melissa.

"Yes, I'm just tired."

"I'm taking her to my room to rest," Logan told his housekeeper, not at all hesitant about letting her know that he and Melissa would be sharing his room.

"I'll be all right," Melissa assured them. "Logan has a cut that needs attention. Do you have a first aid kit or something?"

"There's one in his bathroom." She winked at Melissa. "Don't worry about Logan. He's hard-headed."

"Thanks," he replied dryly.

"You take care of her, Logan. I'll bring you both a pot of tea and something to eat."

Logan took Melissa's hand and led her to his room. Shutting the door behind them, he dragged her against him, desperate to hold her, to taste her, to know she was truly safe.

Melissa pressed her body against Logan's, a shiver running through her as his mouth crashed down on hers. She hung onto him, her hands clutching at his shirt, her heart beating so hard she was sure he could feel it.

He lifted his head. "You risked your life to save me," she whispered into his mouth as he continued to kiss her.

"Thank God I got to you, sweetheart." Despite his gentle tone, anger still simmered inside him. Someone had tried to harm her. Someone evil. Whoever dared to hurt her would answer to him.

She leaned back and touched her hand to his forehead where the blood had dried around his gash. "I need a quick shower and we need to take care of this."

"Shower with me," Logan suggested huskily.

Smiling, she licked her lips. "Mm, I like the sound of that."

Their quick shower turned into a lengthy one as they took turns washing each other, kissing and touching, teasing each other until Melissa could barely stand, her body burning with desire.

After towel-drying her hair, she located the first aid kit under the vanity and set it on the counter. "Sit down," she ordered Logan as she took out the hydrogen peroxide.

Logan's gaze dropped to her perfect breasts, her beaded nipples. "That can wait." He reached for her and she slapped his hand away.

"Sit."

He groaned. "You're awfully bossy for someone who owes me for saving her life."

She rolled her eyes. "Your cut needs tending."

"It's not that bad," he protested. "It's not even bleeding." Seeing she wasn't going to budge on the issue, he begrudgingly sat on the lid of the toilet.

Melissa smiled mischievously, then straddled his lap and sat on his thighs, her body pressed intimately against his engorged manhood. She kissed him. "You be good and let me take care of this and I'll pay you back." Pouring some of the liquid on a gauze pad, she dabbed it on his cut.

Encircling her with his arms, he asked, "Yeah? How do you plan to do that?"

Shifting closer, Melissa grazed his chest with her breasts. "Oh, I'll think of something."

He rolled his hips as his erection grew so hard that he hurt. Their intimate position was killing him. He wanted to be inside her, wanted to keep her beneath him all night long. "Hurry up. I can't take this much longer."

Melissa smiled. "Just a minute."

Logan gritted his teeth. "I'm only human, you little flirt."

She laughed low in her throat as she dabbed his cut one last time. "I think you'll live."

"I'm not so sure." His hands cupped her head, dragged her mouth to his. His tongue delved past her teeth, exploring, tasting, demanding a response.

Twining her arms around his neck, Melissa kissed him back hungrily. His hands gripped her butt as he stood and carried her out of the bathroom. He stopped at the bed and Melissa slithered down his body until her feet found the floor.

A soft knock sounded at the door and she pulled away. "You'd better get that."

He found a tray on the floor outside. He brought it inside, set it on the dresser, then turned toward Melissa. "Are you hungry?" he asked.

"Not for food," she whispered as her gaze traveled boldly over his body.

Logan stared at her, half crazy with wanting her. She was beautiful and sexy and he had to stop himself from going over to her, tossing her on the bed and burying himself deep inside her.

Because he loved her.

He loved her fascinating green eyes, her determination, her strength in the face of danger. He loved looking at her, knowing that he alone could strip her clothing from her and touch her intimately.

Logan's throat went dry as she lay on the bed, then beckoned him with her sexy smile.

"Make love to me, Logan."

He joined her, his mouth taking hers with fierce need. He wanted to make her his in every way—with his mouth, his hands, his body. He wanted her to feel as desperate at the thought of leaving him as he did. He wanted to brand her his in every way possible so when she did leave she would know that no other man would make her feel what he could.

She arched against him as his hands explored her body, moaned as his mouth left hers and trailed kisses down her throat and shoulder to her breast. Sucking gently, he drew her nipple into his mouth, nibbled it with his teeth, savored her taste, her smell, her essence.

He looked at her as she writhed beneath him, watched her eyes glaze with passion as she bit her lower lip. And still he moved lower, kissing her belly, her thighs, between her legs.

Melissa's hips thrashed as Logan's tongue stroked her. Something had changed between them, something emotional and intimate and earth-shattering. The intensity of his lovemaking, of her response to him, took her breath away. Her heart swelled with love as he moved over her.

She welcomed him inside her, tightened her arms around him as he slowly entered her. Opening her legs, she arched upward, wanting more of him than he was giving her. But Logan took his time, filling her ever so slowly. Hot and hard, building on the fire he'd created within her, he teased them both as he withdrew then entered her again. When she thought she could no longer stand it, he answered her unspoken plea and stroked her body with his over and over until they crested the peak of desire together.

Feeling as though she'd never be normal again,

Melissa ran her hands over Logan's back, loving the feel of him on top of her, still inside her. Her heart shifted. She'd known becoming involved with Logan was dangerous, but she'd also known that she couldn't have stopped what was happening between them. And as much as it hurt to think about leaving one day soon, she couldn't regret loving him.

Had she ever stopped loving him?

Tears filled her eyes and she tried her best to stop them. Despite her valiant effort, they spilled down her temples and fell into her hair.

Logan lifted his head and looked at her, his expression one of concern. "What's wrong?"

"Nothing," she told him, hoping he'd believe her. She wasn't surprised when he didn't let the subject drop.

"Are you all right?" he asked, his tone serious and caring. "Did I hurt you?"

She shook her head. "No, I'm fine. Really. It's just…"

I love you.

Clamping her lips together, Melissa stopped herself from blurting out the words.

Logan studied her face, his heart pounding. "What, sweetheart?"

She couldn't tell him. Confessing that she was in love with him would only complicate everything between them. He didn't love her. And once she wrapped up the story, she'd leave. "I guess what happened earlier is finally hitting me."

"It's over now." He kissed her tenderly, then moved to her side and drew her into his arms. He didn't want to let her go. Ever. But he knew in his heart he would have to. He'd asked her to stay once before and she hadn't.

Their circumstances were different now, but the end result would be the same. She lived in Houston. There was a big promotion waiting for her. He knew she had a future in broadcasting and that one day he'd turn on his television to see her anchoring for a major network. He wouldn't be able to live with himself if he stood in her way.

All those years ago he'd been selfish, expecting her to stay in Royal because they were in love. He knew he no longer had the freedom, or the right, to ask that of her. She cared for him, he knew. He could tell by the way she touched him, kissed him.

But that wasn't love—at least not for her.

No, he couldn't ask her to give up everything she'd worked for to stay here. He toyed with the idea of going with her to live in Houston, but knew that would never work.

What would he do in a big city? How long would it be before his missing the hard work of ranching came between them? He was a rancher. Like so many ancestors before him, the dirt of the Wild Spur was in his blood. He'd feel useless anywhere else.

Hell, if he offered to move, would she reject him as she had years ago? No, going with her wasn't an option.

Melissa sighed. "I know. I'm just feeling emotional, I guess."

"That's natural after something traumatic happens."

She turned in his arms, raised herself up on her elbow and propped her head on her hand. "I suppose." Tracing his chin with her finger, she said, "I'm glad you were there, Logan."

"I am, too, sweetheart."

"Do you think Rick will be able to get access to some equipment tomorrow?"

"Yeah, it's probably already set up. I'll call Mark in the morning."

"I'd like to ask another favor, then."

Logan kissed her, then cupped her breast. "Anything you want."

"Mm, that sounds promising," she answered. "But that's not the kind of favor I was thinking of."

He dropped his hand to her hip. "All right, what?"

"I was wondering if your contact at the station would let Rick and me do some work on our story there. Since we're not on a schedule, we could go in any time they'd have the equipment available."

He faked a frown, then laughed. "Just my luck. I have a naked woman in bed with me and she's thinking about work."

Melissa playfully smacked him. "I can always go back to Houston." Afraid of losing what little time she had with him, she hadn't wanted to leave until she was due to return to her job. But she and Rick had a lot of footage so far and she wanted to get some preliminary editing done.

The thought of her leaving, even for a day, made his gut twist. Sitting up, he said, "I don't think it'll be a problem."

"Great!"

"What do I get in return?"

She traced a path down his belly and caressed him.

"I'll think of something," she whispered, then crawled on top of him.

Logan groaned as she scooted down his body, kissing his belly, her tongue wet and hot as she moved lower.

He wondered if she needed any more favors.

"Joe Fisher is the manager of WRYL, your affiliate here," Logan stated at breakfast with Rick and Melissa the next morning. He'd talked to Mark while Melissa was dressing and had learned that arrangements had been made for Rick and Melissa to use the station's facilities. "He's agreed to see you at nine this morning and to set up slots for you to use their equipment while you're putting your story together."

"You're quite the miracle worker," Melissa commented, then gave Logan a sweet, yet seductive smile as she bit into her buttered toast. He'd worked miracles with her in his bed several times during the night.

Rick cleared his throat, breaking the obvious spell between his coworker and his host. "That's great." Swallowing the last of his coffee, he sat back in his chair.

Giving Melissa an impressed look, Logan told her, "Joe recognized your name when Mark mentioned you."

Surprise lit her eyes. "Really?"

"Yeah, he said something about seeing some of your work. Mark said he seemed really interested in meeting you."

"It's nice of him to help us out."

"As soon as you're done, I'll call the sheriff." And the members of the TCC. They were planning to meet to view the video, hoping to recognize the figure.

"I want to go with you to meet with him," Melissa said. "I have some more questions I want to ask him."

Logan had started to speak when his cell phone rang. "Excuse me." He left the room. After a few minutes, he returned and sat. "That was my foreman. There's a fence down and about a hundred head of cattle free." He released a heavy sigh. "I'm going to have to stay here and help round them up." His expression became serious as he looked at Rick. "I want you to stick with Melissa every minute while you're gone."

Rick nodded. "I will. Don't worry about her."

Melissa pushed her plate away. "Okay, you two, I'm sitting right here." She pinned Logan with a stare. "I don't need a keeper."

"I just want you safe. The best way to be sure of that is to have Rick watch out for you."

"I'm not in any danger," she protested.

His lips twisted. "We don't know that for sure."

"But you suspect that the person who caused the accident was after the map. It doesn't make sense that they would harm me."

"You and Rick might have caught the thief on tape," Logan pointed out. "The thief might be responsible for killing Jonathan Devlin and may kill to get the tape. Until we know what's going on, you stay with Rick."

"Do you trust Joe Fisher?" Rick asked.

Logan had known Joe for years. "Yes," he answered without hesitation.

"Then Melissa will be with either Joe or me the entire time we're gone."

"Thanks. And give me a call as soon as you have the tape finished."

Melissa pouted, but that Logan showed his concern for her sent a warm feeling all through her body. "All right," she told him. "You win this time." It was easy to give in to Rick and Logan because, at the moment, she didn't have any plans otherwise. "But I do want to go with you when you talk to the sheriff. And don't even try to talk me out of it."

Ten

"What's going on with you and Logan?" Rick asked, breaking the silence between them as they drove toward WRYL.

"What do you mean?" Melissa asked coyly.

He smiled at her and his eyes twinkled. "Sugar, you're not fooling me with that innocent act. You and the cowboy have been joined at the hip since we arrived."

Blushing, she gave him a sidelong glance. "We're old friends. We're just getting reacquainted."

"Reacquainted in bed?"

"Rick!"

At the honk of a horn, he turned his attention to the road. "Look, the sparks have been flying between you two since the night of the anniversary ball."

"Oh, *pleeeze*." She rolled her eyes.

"The man wanted you that night. It was written all over his face when he walked up to you."

She shook her head and chuckled. "No, actually, I think he wanted to throttle me."

"Not hardly, babe." The song playing on the radio filled the cab for several moments, then Rick looked at her again. "He's been very accommodating since we've arrived."

"Yes, he has," she answered softly. Melissa thought about Rick's comment. Logan *had* been helpful. He'd gone out of his way to be open and friendly. For years she'd mentally forced him into a tiny box that he no longer seemed to fit, and no matter how hard she tried, he wasn't going back into it.

She still didn't want to believe that she was in love with Logan again, but it was silly to deny it. Sighing as Rick turned right off the highway onto the main road that led to the center of Royal, she stared out the window.

Where was her relationship with Logan headed? He hadn't made any promises and she hadn't asked for them. To believe they could have a happily-ever-after ending between them was foolish. In a few days she was going back to her job in Houston. Back to where she belonged.

But after being here with Logan, living in Houston seemed a lifetime ago. She'd once thrived on the excitement of a big city, relished her work as a reporter, looked forward to achieving even more success with her job.

Now she knew they were only replacements for what was lacking in her life.

Love.

Fulfillment.

Logan.

Maybe her heart would survive the trauma of living without him.

She remained silent as Rick parked in the lot at the television station. One thing she couldn't seem to stop thinking about: she'd never been happier.

Getting out of the truck, Melissa waited for Rick to retrieve his camera from behind his seat.

She *was* happy with Logan. She loved him deeply, cherished each moment with him. But that didn't mean they had a future together, did it?

She'd said as much to Logan when she'd pointed out they led separate lives. He hadn't corrected her, hadn't tried to make more of their relationship than the physical love they shared. That, more than anything, told her how he felt.

Yes, she loved him, but he didn't feel the same.

So where did that leave her?

Joe Fisher was waiting for Melissa and Rick when they entered the lobby. About fifteen years older than her, Joe was balding and had the kindest blue eyes of anyone she'd ever met. "Hi. I'm Melissa Mason. This is my videographer, Rick."

"You don't need an introduction," Joe said with a cordial smile. "I know exactly who you are. It's so nice to meet you. And you, Rick. Please come this way.

"Do you have time for a quick tour of the station?" he asked.

"We'd love one," Melissa answered for them. She could hardly say no, and besides, she'd been impressed by the décor. It was both professional and attractive.

The station was smaller than theirs in Houston, but the technology was state of the art. Melissa complimented him.

"We're quite proud of it."

Joe led them through the engineering department and showed them the editing facilities. "Make yourself at home. If you have any questions, there's an assistant production coordinator in the next room."

An hour later they were done copying the accident video. They left with two tapes: one for them and one for Logan. As they drove to the ranch, Melissa called Logan to let him know they were returning. He was standing in the driveway when they pulled up. Rick dropped her off, then backed his truck up and drove to his cottage.

Melissa held out one of the tapes as she approached Logan, but instead of taking it he pulled her to him and kissed her. For an insane moment, she allowed herself to fantasize what it would be like to be greeted with his kisses for the rest of her life, to live on his ranch, to have his love for eternity.

Aware that wasn't going to happen, she banished the longing from her heart and kissed him back, telling herself she should be grateful for having the time with him now.

"Mmm, that was nice. Care to take this inside?" Melissa whispered when Logan lifted his mouth from hers.

Logan could think of nothing he'd like more. The thought of making love to Melissa consumed him. Day and night.

What's happened between us is wonderful, but it can't last. We both know it.

Melissa's words haunted him. She'd made it clear she wasn't expecting more than an affair. His gut twisted. For her, their affair was just about the sex.

He didn't have her heart.

"There's nothing I'd like more, but I have a meeting at the club in thirty minutes." He moved his hips against hers, the bulge in his jeans pressing against her belly.

"Really?"

Taking the tape, he said, "We're going to view this to see if anyone recognizes the blurred image of the person taking the map."

"I want to go with you." Melissa held Logan's gaze. "I know Gavin will be there. I want to talk with him to see if he's learned anything more about what happened at the museum."

"I'll ask him for you. I know he has another meeting to go to after this one. Maybe he can talk with you later today.

"I hope so."

"I don't want you waiting in the truck and you won't be allowed inside," he told her. "The club is for members only."

She snorted. "No women allowed? What kind of things go on inside there, anyway?" she asked.

He grinned engagingly. "Curious, huh?"

"As you said to Gavin, I'm a reporter. Maybe I'll do a story on it."

Logan knew she was teasing by her playful expression but couldn't stop the discouragement from coming out. "I don't think that would be a good idea, sweetheart."

"What? You don't want the world to know that you're heroes who thwart crime and save damsels in distress?"

"Heroes?" He laughed easily. "You have quite an imagination."

Melissa studied his expression and found it just a little too practiced. "My imagination is fine. As a matter of fact, I'm imagining myself naked, crawling on top of you and—"

"Stop it, you're killing me," he said with a groan. Torn between duty and desire, he glanced at his watch. He cursed when he realized he had just enough time to get to his meeting. He kissed her pouty lips. "I really do have to go, Melissa."

"All right," she said with frustration that was a little bit fake and a whole lot real. "Your loss."

"I'll make it up to you when I get back," he promised.

"I'm going to hold you to that."

He grinned as she moved out of his arms. "I was hoping you would."

Mark Hartman was the last member to arrive. Though he walked in only minutes after Logan, who had just taken a seat a the conference table, he still got a good ribbing from his friends for being five minutes late.

"Nice of you to join us," Connor quipped, rocking back on two legs of his chair.

"Yeah, it's not like we don't have other things to do," Jake added with a laugh.

Mark frowned. "All right, knock it off. I've lost another nanny and I haven't had any luck finding a replacement." He plopped into his chair and slumped down, looking both frustrated and worn out.

"Someone will turn up," Logan offered.

Concern etched his features. "Yeah, but in the meantime my niece is having to adjust to temporary sitters. The self-defense studio is thriving and I need someone I can count on, someone who doesn't mind taking care of her on the spur of the moment."

Tom gave him a reassuring look. "It's not like you planned to raise a child. Losing your brother and sister-in-law unexpectedly was hard enough. Not everyone would have stepped up to raise their niece."

"Yeah," Jake chimed in. "We all know how much you love her. You're doing the right thing. Give it some time. It'll work out."

Standing, Logan walked to the corner of the room and fed the tape Melissa had given him into the video recorder connected to large television. "Let's get down to business. You've all heard about the incident at the museum by now?"

"So the map hasn't turned up yet?" Mark asked, still feeling responsible since he'd was supposed to have been guarding it.

"No," Gavin said. "Melissa was nearly killed and we believe it was because of the map."

Connor brought his chair down on all four legs. "So you don't think Melissa was the target?"

"No. But someone wanted the map desperately enough to kill for it. Jonathan Devlin's murder proved that. This latest incident confirms how bold the killer is.

If Logan hadn't gotten to her when he did, Melissa could have died."

Just hearing Gavin state the killer's intent caused Logan's blood to boil. "Which means that if she wasn't the original target, she might be one now. Whoever did this might think they were caught on tape stealing the map. Or, that possibly they were seen by her."

Jake swore. "Is Melissa all right?"

Logan nodded. "She's a little bruised, but she says she's fine." Pride filled him. "She's taking the ordeal like a trooper and continuing to cover the story." He didn't like it, but he respected her dedication to her job. "I'm going to make damn sure nothing happens to her again."

A brief moment of silence followed Logan's declaration, then Mark asked, "Do you know how the chandelier broke loose?"

"Someone definitely tampered with the wiring and the bolts. It was rigged to drop. We haven't determined how anyone could have gotten access to the attic to do so, but we're still investigating," Gavin explained.

Logan hit the play button. The museum room appeared on the screen, the map on the podium in the center. "This is the tape from the accident. We were lucky to capture some of it. Unfortunately, where the killer comes in is blurred because the cameraman got bumped during the melee. But it's obvious that someone comes near the podium after the chandelier fell. That individual has to be the person who stole the map."

The men studied the television in silence. After showing it once, Logan hit the rewind button and they viewed it a second time. "The person isn't very tall."

Connor nodded in agreement. "I think it's a woman. The figure seems too small to be a man."

"Logan, play it again and stop it when the image moves into view," Jake said. As the tape started playing, he walked over to the television. "Stop."

Logan stopped the tape.

Jake pointed to the slender, blurred image. "It's a woman, for sure. Look at the head." He circled a small section with his finger. "She has a black cap on, but her hair is in a ponytail. See here?"

"You're right." Gavin's eyes never left the screen. "The color of her hair is either light brown or blond. But I can't make out who she is. Does anyone recognize her?"

Mark shook his head. "She doesn't look familiar to me."

"Me, either," Logan added. "Wait." He placed his finger against the screen. "There are letters on the cap. See? There's an *S* and a *C*."

Connor frowned, then said, "That's odd. Why would it have letters that far apart? Look here, her ponytail is between the two letters. There's probably more beneath it."

"I think you're right, Connor," Gavin agreed. "At least we now have something to go on. We agree it's a woman?" he asked. They all nodded. "And the letters on her black cap are an *S* and a *C*?" He rubbed his hand over his jaw. "Unfortunately her description fits about a third of the women of Royal."

Satisfied they'd gotten a solid lead, Logan turned off the television, then removed the tape from the recorder. "What's happening out at the Windcroft horse farm?" he asked Gavin, referring to the trouble Nita Windcroft had been complaining about. "Anything turn up about the poisoned horse feed?"

Gavin took a deep breath. "Nita's confirmed that the feed didn't come from her regular supplier. In addition to the cut fences she's already reported, she called me this morning with another complaint. She said the air had been let out of the tires in several of her horse trailers. She's convinced that a Devlin is behind the mischief going out there."

Mark sat forward. "What do you think?"

"That she may be right, but with no actual proof, my hands are tied. We need to consider sending someone out to her horse farm to keep an eye on things."

"If we do," Logan interjected, "it may look like we're taking sides."

"Right. The Devlins might believe we're already suspecting them," Jake said.

"Which could put fire under the feud if they're innocent," Connor reasoned.

"It may be wise to hold off sending anyone anywhere until we have more to go on," Mark suggested. "Nita should understand that."

"She mentioned that she'd heard that Jonathan Devlin was murdered, which only raised her suspicions that the Devlins have something to do with her problems."

"One of us could talk to Lucas," Tom suggested. "That might be enough to calm her down."

"Good idea," Gavin agreed. "But since you're just getting acquainted with your family, let's keep you out of it."

"I could go to see Lucas and his family and ask a few

questions," Logan offered. "I won't suggest the Devlins are behind anything, but it would interesting to gauge their reactions to all of this."

Gavin nodded. "That's a good idea. We'll meet after you've talked to Lucas. In the meantime, everyone keep an eye out for a woman matching our suspect's description. So far she's our best lead in solving this mystery. And Logan, stay close to Melissa. We don't know yet if she's in danger."

Logan nodded, but he'd already made that decision. Someone was going to be with her whenever she was away from the ranch. Whether she liked it or not.

Two days later Melissa sat back in her chair at WRYL's editing facilities and smiled at Rick. "We're done with this part of our story."

"The editing went faster than I anticipated," Rick said.

"Yes. I need to talk to the sheriff to see if he has anything more on the Devlin murder." If something concrete didn't turn up soon, she'd have to start digging more into Jessamine's past. Melissa had already delved into the story about the gold heist Jessamine had engineered. In the process, Melissa had read something about Jessamine possibly being involved with a man—the town sheriff. Supposedly they'd had a love affair, but Melissa hadn't been able to discover if it was true or what had happened between them.

But if Jessamine had suffered a broken romance, Melissa knew how she felt. Her own heart ached at the thought of leaving Logan.

You knew it was only an affair, her mind taunted.

She'd told herself that she could enjoy being with him temporarily, that she could deal with a brief affair.

She'd been wrong.

Sighing, she stood. "I'm going to find Joe and thank him for giving us access to their equipment. I'll let him know we're finished."

She found Joe in his office. When he saw her at his door, he waved her inside. "Rick and I want to thank you again for the use of your facilities."

Joe nodded. "You're more than welcome. Come back if you need to."

She and Rick had finished editing all the footage they had so far. But Gavin had promised to keep her updated on his investigation, so it was possible she'd need access to the studio again.

She and Joe spent a few minutes chatting. He asked her about her career, and Melissa told him a little about her work. He seemed quite interested and even mentioned a documentary she'd done on battered women which had won an industry award. She was surprised he even knew about it.

Joe stood. "I enjoyed talking with you."

"It's been a pleasure." Melissa smiled and shook Joe's hand as she started to leave.

"Look, I can't let this opportunity go by without mentioning that I'd be interested in talking with you about working at WRYL." He took out his card and handed it to her.

"I don't know, I—"

"Oh, I know there's less prestige working in Royal and the pay wouldn't match what you make in Houston because we're a smaller market, but we'd do our best to make it up in perks."

"Thank you. I appreciate your interest."

"Feel free to call me anytime," he said, coming around his desk. He walked with her back to the editing facility. Rick appeared to be waiting for her, his camera and a couple of tapes in his hands. He handed them to her as she approached and she tucked them into her bag.

As they left, Melissa thought about the differences between her station in Houston and this smaller one in Royal. The pace was definitely slower here. She'd had the chance to catch a couple of their newscasts and found their presentation was topnotch, their field reporters professional. The quality of her work certainly wouldn't be jeopardized in the smaller market.

In Houston she lived and breathed her job, rushing to assignments, racing to meet deadlines. All of that effort built her profile so that, one day, she could see herself working for a major news network. That's what her focus in life up to now had been. And, she was on the verge of a major promotion.

Could she even consider staying in Royal? Could she slow down her professional pace and start filling in all those pieces—home, family…love—that had been missing in her life? Could she make a commitment to Logan?

For a moment her heart soared with the possibility of marrying him. She would be greeted by his kisses the way she'd dreamed the other day. She would love him, and he would… Her thoughts paused there. She didn't know if Logan loved her or not. He desired her, yes. But did he love her? Was she really considering changing her career path without the certainty of a future with him?

Because one thing *was* certain, for her career, it would be a move in the wrong direction.

Eleven

"He's beautiful." Melissa laughed as the young calf trotted after his mother in one of the Wild Spur's pastures. Needing to check his stock, Logan had invited her for a tour of his ranch.

Another week had passed. Daniel had called to ask how things were coming along. Melissa had done more research on the town of Royal than she'd ever dreamed she would. She and Rick had spent hours looking at newspapers on microfiche. Sheriff O'Neal had given her another interview, which Rick had filmed.

Today they were both taking a day off. Sharing Logan's love for his ranch, she was glad for the opportunity to ride along with him.

Leaning against the split rail fence, Logan propped his foot on the bottom rail. "He's from prime stock. His father's a descendent in a line of champions. In the future, I'll use that little bull to breed."

Logan's future—one that didn't include her.

Hearing him say the word stopped her heart. She looked around at the never-ending expanse of land, felt the warmth of the sun shining down on her, heating her skin. Yet inside she suddenly was chilled.

When she'd decided to take this assignment and return to Royal, she'd dreaded the thought of seeing him again. She'd never conceived that they would have anything other than animosity between them, let alone enter into an affair.

Amazingly, they'd managed to work through the pain of their past. Though they'd discovered that they had been manipulated by his brother and Cara, their fragile intimacy didn't change the stark truth of reality.

Logan had said he loved her years ago. She'd wanted to believe it. But he'd married another woman shortly after she'd left. If he'd fallen in love with Cara so soon after she'd moved to Houston, could he have truly loved her? Needing to hear his explanation, she rested her arm on the fence. "Logan, I know we talked about this before, but I need to hear some things again…get them straight in my mind." She took a deep breath, struggling to find the courage to speak further. Then she finally faced him. "Did you love Cara?" She braced herself for his answer.

Ever since that night they'd confronted their past, Logan had dreaded this moment. He didn't want to hurt her, but how could he explain why he'd fallen so easily for Cara? "When I married her I thought I did," he answered, his voice carrying an edge of anger at Bart's and

Cara's deception. "And that didn't happen until six months after you'd left."

"Six months." Disappointment and anger flashed through Melissa. Not long to grieve for a broken engagement with a woman he'd professed to love, a woman he'd planned to spend the rest of his life with. "Why didn't you call me?"

"Pride, I guess. And anger." Bitterness mixed with regret in his tone. "I was so damn angry with you." Hurt flickered through her eyes, and he hated being the one who caused it.

"That doesn't say a lot for your love for me, Logan," she responded bluntly.

Heat flushed Logan's cheeks. "Your rejection stung, hitting me where I was most vulnerable." A few moments passed before he forced himself to continue. "After my mother died, I didn't have anyone in my life who really cared about me. Until you."

"And I left you." She couldn't ignore that she'd played a part in their bitter breakup. Young and naive, she hadn't trusted her own instincts, her own love for Logan.

He shrugged as if it didn't matter, but it had. "Cara came into my life at my lowest point. To be honest, she pursued me, made me feel special. She began talking about marriage and I thought, why the hell not?"

"It wasn't long before I realized I'd married Cara on the rebound from loving you. I missed you and I thought I'd never feel whole again. They were all the wrong reasons for marriage. I felt awful and, as the weeks passed, I faced the fact that it wasn't going to work between us. We got divorced within a year. She didn't even fight it—

just took her settlement and walked." He gave a hard laugh. "Now, aware of her and Bart's association, I know why."

"Somehow that makes me feel a little better." Though she accepted that he'd fallen for another woman and had married quickly, it still hurt. But she needed to move past her resentment to heal her spirit. She knew now that she had to give him her trust.

He expelled a harsh breath. "It makes me feel like an idiot."

"You weren't an idiot. You were fooled by Cara." She laid her hand on his arm. "We both were."

"And I was lonely," he told her. "I wanted you and couldn't have you."

Sadness stole over her expression as she withdrew her hand. "I wish we could go back."

"We can't, though, sweetheart." He wrapped his arms around her and tucked her head against his shoulder. She tilted her face and his gaze drifted over her, taking in the shadows in her eyes, the pain. "It took me years to get over you."

Melissa sighed as he held her. But he had gotten over her. He'd moved on with his life. She leaned up on her toes and kissed him. "At least we both know the truth, Logan. Though it can't make up for the past, we've had this time together."

"You're amazing. Only you could find something good in the tragedy of our past." Amazing was how she felt in his arms. Logan tightened his embrace.

Stepping back, she favored him with a smile. "I bet you say that to all the girls."

He chuckled. "There haven't been many. My attempts at dating haven't gone very well," he admitted. "No one could take your place."

She blushed. "That a sweet thing to say."

Unable to stop himself, he asked, "What about you? Has there been someone special in your life?"

Shaking her head, she met his gaze. "When I first started working I didn't have time in my life for a relationship. Later, I dated someone I cared about, but he resented my work and…" Unable to tell him the whole truth, she let her words drop off.

Because I loved you. I always will.

Melissa turned away, not wanting him to read her thoughts.

Logan glanced at his watch. "We'd better get back to the house. I have a meeting with Lucas at the Devlins' ranch."

She entwined her hand with his and they walked to the truck Logan used on the ranch. Old and a little beat-up, its red paint was covered in several layers of dust, but the ride out to the pasture had been smooth. "What are you going to see him about?"

"Nita Windcroft insists the Devlins are behind some trouble she's been having out at her horse farm. Recently she found flat tires on several of her horse trailers. She's also had downed fences and their line shack broken into."

"So you're going to see Lucas to ask him if his family is causing the problems?"

He started driving toward the house. "Not in those words. The last thing anyone wants is to encourage trouble between the Devlins and the Windcrofts. I'm going more to see if I can shed any light on it."

"Great. I'll go with you."

Logan gave her a sidelong glance, observed the determination written on her face. "You're staying at the ranch, sweetheart."

Melissa glared at him. "Why?"

Pulling into the yard, he stopped the truck short, his mind made up. There was no way in hell he was taking her with him. After the accident with the chandelier, he wasn't placing her in any further danger. "Because."

"That's not an answer, Logan."

Because I love you.

But he couldn't admit that. She'd already told him one relationship had failed because of jealousy over her work. He wasn't going to make her feel guilty for making that choice.

"Because of the accident that almost took your life," he finally said. "Besides, if you go along, Lucas may not be as open to discussing what's been going on at the Windcrofts'." Logan reached across her and opened her door. "I respect what you do, Melissa, but I want you safe. I'm going to the Devlin ranch alone. With all that's been happening, I don't know what I'm going to be walking into." He nodded. "I'll be back in an hour and tell you what I learned."

"Can you at least ask Lucas if I can talk to him?"

"That I'll do. Stay here until I get back. There are a lot of hands around here who would notice anything suspicious in my absence." It was an order. He could tell she didn't like it, but if it kept her safe, that was what mattered.

Melissa didn't think anyone was after her, but she could tell she'd never convince Logan of that. Giving in, she said, "All right. I'll see you in a little while." Without waiting for a response, she shut the door, then headed for the house.

As Logan pulled out of the yard, he caught a glimpse of her in his rearview mirror as she disappeared inside. He hadn't meant to be curt, but hell, he was worried for her safety. Couldn't she see that?

If something happened to her while she was here, he'd never get over it. Maybe he couldn't protect her in Houston, but here in Royal he could. Whether she liked it or not.

Houston.

Logan knew that the more information she gathered, the closer the time came when she'd be leaving. Having her talk to Lucas at a later date would buy him a few more days with her.

But she didn't have to know that, did she?

Trying to put thoughts of Melissa out of his mind, Logan crossed the cattle guard and drove up the dirt road toward Lucas's house. The large brick-and-frame structure only hinted at the wealth of the family living inside. Stopping the truck, he cut the engine, got out and went to the door.

He hoped the Windcrofts and Devlins could find a peaceable solution. But if the past was anything to go by, he had his doubts.

As Melissa worked on her story in her room, her cell phone rang. She glanced at her watch before answering, surprised to find thirty minutes had passed. She frowned when her producer's name flashed on her caller ID.

"Hi, Daniel, what's up?"

"How's the story out there coming along?"

"There have been some new developments."

"Great. You can fill me in when you get back. I've got some news for you," he said, his voice excited. "Your promotion has come through. We're ready to put you on the air."

"What?" Melissa's pulse quickened.

"I want you to wrap up your work there and get back here by tomorrow."

His words caught her by surprise. Instead of the elation she'd expected at reaching her goal, panic swept through her. "Wait a minute. What are you talking about?"

"We're putting you on the air this weekend. You and Rick need to leave for Houston right away to be back here no later than tomorrow afternoon," he ordered.

"Tomorrow?" Stunned, she stared at her notes. "But I'm still looking into Jessamine Golden's legend. As a matter of fact, there's been a murder in town and there's a possible connection to Jessamine's map."

"Don't worry about that."

"I've put a lot into this story, Daniel," she said desperately. "It's only fair that I finish covering it."

"The story's all yours. You can keep updated on the investigation through phone calls from here. If need be, we can send someone else there to do your leg work."

A beep sounded from her phone, and she groaned

when she realized the battery was low. “Look, Daniel, my phone’s going to die. Let me call you back.”

“Don’t bother. Explain to Rick what’s up and you two get back here stat. And congratulations!”

“Daniel—” Melissa stared at her phone in disbelief when it lost the connection. Her promotion had come through. By the weekend she’d be on the air as a news anchor. She’d have everything she wanted, everything she’d worked for.

But if that was true, why did she feel so miserable?

She set her phone in its cradle to charge, then sat back against the headboard of the bed. As she always known it would, the time had come for her to leave. Now, every single minute she could be with Logan counted. She wanted him here with her, wanted to spend her last evening with him in bed.

Touching him.

Kissing him.

Making love with him.

Except he wasn’t here.

But she knew where he was. She’d go to the Devlin ranch. Logan had taken the ranch truck, but the keys to his pickup were on the foyer table. All she needed were the directions. Melissa hurried out of her bedroom to find Norah.

A few minutes later, Melissa drove away from the ranch. On the way to the Devlin’s, she kept an eye out for Logan, hoping she’d see him and be able to flag him down. He’d been far enough ahead of her to have possibly finished his business and be heading home.

Seeing the name of the road Norah had given her,

Melissa turned off the main highway. She bumped along, then spotted a chimney standing alone on a hill signaling the entrance to the Devlin ranch.

As she turned right at a post with an iron D-V brand on it, she heard a sharp crack and something exploded through the passenger window of the truck. Screaming, she slammed on the brakes and jerked the wheel to the right. The truck lurched to the side of the road, nearly running into a ditch. Ducking, she pressed her face against the seat.

Someone was shooting at her!

The metallic taste of fear coated her throat. "Ohmygodohmygodohmygod!" Her heart slammed against her rib cage.

Were they still out there? Would they approach the truck to make sure she was dead? Logan had told her to stay home. Why hadn't she listened to him?

Oh, God, she was going to die here. And if she didn't, Logan was going to kill her when he saw her. Her hand shook as she frantically searched through her purse. Where was her damn cell phone! She groaned, remembering she'd left it at the ranch, charging.

Think, Melissa, think!

Looking around the inside of the cab she saw Logan's CB radio.

Thank God!

She turned it on and the radio squawked to life. Grabbing the handset, she pressed the side button and shouted, "I don't know if anyone's out there, but I need help! Someone's shooting at me." Releasing the button, she fought for calm as she listened to see if anyone had heard her. Though there hadn't been any more shots, she wasn't about to stick her head up and risk becoming a target.

Her ears still humming from the sound of the bullet piercing the glass, she looked up. The window on the passenger side had a spider-web effect, with a hole the size of a bottle cap in the glass.

When the radio remained silent, she tried again. "Help! This is Melissa Mason. I'm in Logan Voss's truck at the entrance to Lucas Devlin's ranch. Someone shot at the passenger window. I need help!"

"Melissa?"

"Yes!" *Oh, God.* "Hello, can you hear me?" She wasn't sure who was speaking, but she knew she'd heard his voice before. "Who is this?"

"Melissa, this is Mark Hartman. I'm with Jake Thorne."

"Thank God." They were Logan's friends. She could trust them. "Don't lose me," she begged.

"I'm not going to lose you, Melissa," Mark stated, his voice composed and encouraging. "But I need you to calm down and tell me where you are again. This time slowly."

Her nerves shattered, Melissa bit her lip as she tried to collect herself. "Mark, I'm in Logan's truck at the entrance to Lucas Devlin's ranch. Someone shot at me," she said, her voice trembling.

"Are you hurt?" Mark asked.

"N-no. I'm just scared."

"Okay. Now listen to me, Melissa. Jake and I aren't far from you. We'll be there in a few minutes. Stay down until we get to you. Understand?"

"Y-yes. I will. Hurry, please!" Clutching the microphone in her hand, she prayed they'd get to her quickly.

As Logan walked out of Lucas's home, he ran into Tom Morgan who lived in a guest house on the property. "Your uncle insisted your family has nothing to do with the trouble out at the Windcroft farm," Logan told Tom.

"That's pretty much what I expected him to say. Thanks for coming out, though."

"I hope things will quiet down." He started for his pickup. "I need to be heading back. Melissa's waiting for me." At least she'd stayed at home. With her determination to get a story, he'd half expected her to show up at the Devlin's ranch. With a sigh, Logan opened his door.

"N-no. I'm just scared," a voice cried out on his radio.

"Okay. Now listen to me, Melissa. Jake and I aren't far from you. We'll be there in a few minutes. Stay down until we get to you. Understand?"

Logan froze. Melissa? That couldn't be possible. She was back at the house waiting for him.

"Y-yes. I will. Hurry, please!"

"God, that's Melissa!" Logan shouted. Jumping into the truck, he snatched up the microphone. "Melissa, this is Logan. Where are you?"

"Logan!" Melissa screamed, her voice raw with fear. "I'm at the entrance to the Devlin ranch. I'm in your truck. Someone shot at me. The passenger window's shattered."

He muttered an oath. "Are you all right?" he demanded, his chest feeling as if it might explode.

"Yes, I'm just scared. I wasn't hurt."

Logan turned the key and the engine roared to life. “I’ll be right there, sweetheart. Stay put and stay down!”

“Please hurry,” she whispered, her teeth chattering as icy fear traveled down her spine.

“I’m going with you,” Tom said, dashing around to the other side of Logan’s pickup. He’d barely made it inside before Logan floored it. Rocks and dirt flew in their wake as the vehicle bolted down the dirt road.

“Logan, this is Mark,” his friend said over the CB. “Jake and I are about five minutes away.”

“Thanks, guys. I’m closer, maybe two minutes from her. I’ll meet you. Keep an eye out for anyone suspicious on your way.” He turned his attention to Melissa. “Sweetheart, can you hear me?”

“Yes, Logan. I can hear you.”

“I’m almost there.” The vehicle rounded a curve practically on two wheels. Logan spotted his pickup parked at an angle off the dirt road. “I can see you now. Have you heard any more shots?”

“No.”

“I’ll be there in seconds,” he promised. He’d never heard her sound so terrified.

As he came out of the turn, he stomped on the accelerator. The tires kicked up clouds of dust as it shot down the road toward her. When they got close enough, Logan slammed on the brakes and jerked the pickup to a stop. Jumping out, he raced toward her, Tom hot on his heels. He yanked open the door, then reached inside and gathered Melissa into his arms.

“Melissa, sweetheart, are you okay?” Logan’s body sheltered hers as he held her tight against him.

Relieved to be in Logan's arms, Melissa clung to him. "Yes," she said breathlessly, her body trembling.

Another vehicle pulled up. Mark and Jake hopped out and ran toward them.

"Is she all right?" Jake asked.

"I think so," Logan called back.

"Stay low while we check around," Mark told them.

Logan held Melissa and calmed her as Jake, Mark and Tom, armed with rifles, investigated the surrounding area.

Melissa stayed by Logan's side as she repeated her story, explaining the shot had come as she was turning onto the dirt road.

Searching Melissa's face, Logan kissed her. "God, I was scared to death when I heard you on the radio. Are you sure you're not hurt?"

Burrowing closer to him, she whispered, "No, but I'm glad you were nearby."

"What were you doing out here? I thought I told you to wait at the house for me?" He silently berated himself for leaving her behind. If he hadn't, this wouldn't have happened.

She met his gaze and the intensity of it shocked her. "I know you did. I just wanted to tell you that Daniel called. He wants me to—"

His muscles tensed. *Her job.* "You risked your life for a story."

She searched his tight expression. "No, Logan, it's not like that. I've faced difficult situations in the past, but I—"

"So this is nothing new," he cut in, annoyance creeping into his tone. "You put yourself in danger all the time." He knew her job was demanding, but the awareness she'd almost been killed twice—both in relation to him—made him shake with alarm.

Melissa stared at him in silence, thinking it was best if she left as soon as possible. Logan would never have to know that she'd been coming for him.

He didn't love her. His disparaging tone told her that. Her last-minute attempt to be with him was only putting off the inevitable. Logan wasn't going to ask her to stay.

Taking a breath, she said, "Some stories are more risky than others." Melissa didn't know where the strength to say the words came from. "I've been in some pretty tough circumstances before, but I've never been shot at."

His eyes narrowed. "Doesn't that bother you?"

"Yes, it does," she admitted. "I try not to think about it. It's a risk every reporter takes."

He set her away from him. "But the risk doesn't stop you from investigating?"

She shook her head, her words coming harder than she'd planned. "I do what I'm assigned. I don't always get to pick and choose. I've worked for a long time to earn a promotion. This story is my ticket."

"Your work is that important to you, isn't it?" he asked.

She looked him straight in the eyes, knowing that without Logan, her work was all she had. "Yes, it is. As a matter of fact, Daniel wants me back in Houston tomorrow. My promotion came through. I'm going to be a news anchor beginning this weekend."

"I see." His lips compressing, Logan felt as though

he was being ripped open. She'd been waiting for this call. It was time for her to leave Royal.

And him.

Someone cleared his throat and they both turned to see Mark, Jake and Tom standing behind them. Logan felt his face flame with heat as he took in the speculative looks on their faces. "Did you find anything?" he asked, hoping to stave off comments about what they'd heard.

"No. It appears the shot came from across the road in those woods," Jake said, pointing in that direction.

"Whoever it was is long gone," Mark added.

"Why would they have shot at me?" Melissa asked. "I don't know anything."

Tom shoved his hands in his pockets. "I'm not sure they were shooting at you. Since it was Logan's vehicle, whoever did this might have thought he was driving," he suggested. "They might have done this to scare Logan off."

She frowned. "Why?"

"We're trying to settle things between the Devlins and the Windcrofts. It looks like someone is doing their best to make sure that doesn't happen. The reason is still a mystery." Jake looked at Logan. "What did Lucas have to say?"

"He claims his family isn't responsible for anything happening at the Windcrofts' and he'd like nothing better than to see the feud between the two families settled for good."

"Did he know anything about the map?" Mark asked.

"Only that it had been stolen. He doesn't believe a Devlin had anything to do with it."

Melissa looked away from Logan. "So you still don't know who took the map?" she asked Mark.

"No, but we're showing the picture around. We'll find the woman who took it."

Though interested in learning the details, Melissa found her mind couldn't focus. All she wanted to do was return home with Logan and curl up in the safety of his arms. Instead, she had to face reality and pack.

She extended her hand, her fingers still trembling. "Thank you so much for coming to my aid. I really appreciate it."

Mark briefly shook her hand. "No problem, Melissa. We're glad you're okay." He shot a look at Logan. "You have this under control, buddy?" he asked.

Logan glowered at them. "Yeah. Tom—"

"I'll drive this truck to my place, Logan," Tom said, reading his thoughts. "You can get it tomorrow. I'll also call Gavin and report what happened."

"Thanks." Hustling Melissa to his ranch truck, Logan helped her inside, then climbed behind the wheel, started the engine and stepped on the accelerator, flying past Mark and Jake who were just getting into Mark's vehicle.

You don't have that right.

No, he didn't.

They were lovers. Nothing more.

Since her return to Royal, she'd made it perfectly clear her life, job and future were in Houston.

You love her.

Yeah, he did. But he wasn't part of her equation, was he? He wrestled with telling her how much she meant to him, telling her that he couldn't live without her.

Asking her to stay.

Begging her to marry him. To live with him here. To have his children. He could easily imagine her with their child in her arms. A little girl with her mother's beautiful green eyes.

God, how could she even think of leaving? They'd lost many years of being together, loving each other, sharing ups and downs—endless nights of making love.

Over the past few weeks, they'd recaptured part of their past, but it hadn't changed the present course of their lives. He toyed briefly with the idea of combining their worlds, but in his heart he knew that would never work. She didn't belong here on the Wild Spur any more than he belonged in Houston. And he couldn't operate his ranch long-distance. He had no right to hold on to his dreams and ask her to let go of hers.

"When do you have to leave?" he forced himself to ask, breaking the tense silence between them.

Melissa looked at Logan and shuddered. His hands were nearly white as he gripped the steering wheel, and he hadn't even looked at her when he'd spoken. She turned her head and stared out the window. He was so handsome, so strong, so confident and in control.

She wished she felt the same way.

But she didn't. When Logan had walked up to her at the anniversary ball, her entire existence had changed. She'd never stood a chance.

Leaving him years ago had broken her heart. Over time, she'd picked up the pieces and vowed never again to allow herself to be hurt. But the pain she'd endured then was nothing compared to the pain ravaging her soul at this moment.

"In about an hour." It cost her dearly to say the words. Though Daniel had said to be in Houston by tomorrow, Logan didn't know that. With everything between them, there was no way she could postpone her departure until the morning. She needed a clean break. It was the only chance she had of leaving Royal in one piece. "I'll pack my things as soon as we get back."

"I see." Logan could barely squeeze the words past the knot in his throat. What they'd shared the past few weeks came down to one final hour together. He didn't want to spend the time at odds with her. Pulling into his driveway, he parked his truck and turned off the key. "Is there anything you need help with?" he asked in an effort to diffuse the strain between them.

Melissa shook her head. "No, I don't have that much to do." Opening her door, she got out. They walked inside together. As they stepped into the house, she turned and said, "Logan, I'm really sorry about your truck. I'll pay for the damages."

A frown creased his brow. "You think I'm upset about

the damn truck?" he growled. He embraced her. "Ah, sweetheart, come here. Melissa, I'm not angry at you."

She looked up at him, her eyes searching his. "You're not?"

"I'm just having a hard time accepting that your job puts you in danger." A harder time believing that it didn't bother her.

Melissa caught her breath, realizing she'd pulled off her ruse quite well. He'd believed her when she'd said it was her job sometimes to walk on the edge of danger. "Oh."

His arms tightened around her. "And I guess I always knew the time would come when you'd leave." His chest rumbled with quiet laughter. "Being with you for the past couple of weeks was worth the worry you put me through."

Pulling away, Melissa looked up at him, her fingers playing with the button on his shirt. "Thanks, I think." She smiled, then pressed her lips together to maintain her composure. "It's been wonderful, Logan. I'll never forget you."

His gaze met hers. "I want you to know I respect what you do, and I'm proud of you." She was an amazing reporter. He couldn't resent that she loved her work.

"You'll never know how much that means to me." Unsteady, she stepped out of his arms before she broke down and made a fool of herself. "I'd better start packing,"

He nodded and she walked away, step by fragile step. Her vision blurred. By sheer will, she reached her room and shut the door. Leaning against the solid, cold wood, she cried.

This time when she left, it would be permanent.

She'd never hold Logan again. As she dried her eyes, she told herself how fortunate she'd been to have the chance to be with him once more. It had been wonderful—more thrilling than she could ever have dreamed.

Numb, she called Rick, discussed Daniel's call and his request that they return to Houston, then told him she'd be ready in an hour. She stored her phone in her purse, and gathered her clothes. What didn't fit in the one bag she'd brought with her, she stuffed in the shopping bags she'd kept. Finished, she glanced around the room to be sure she wasn't leaving anything behind.

But she was.

Logan.

Every single fiber of her revolted at the thought of never seeing him again.

And then she could no longer hold it inside. Tears flowed hot and fast as she sobbed with soul-deep agony. She buried her face into the bed covers to muffle the sounds of her pain and cried until there was nothing left inside her.

Until she lay exhausted and emotionally spent.

A tap on her door had her sitting up and wiping her eyes.

"You ready?"

"One minute," she replied to Rick, surprised at how calm she sounded when her life was falling apart. At least it wasn't Logan. She doubted she could have handled him now.

With what little life was left in her, she went into the bathroom, washed her face, then repaired her makeup.

Anyone looking at her would attribute her paleness to the shooting, not her heart breaking.

Now, all she had left to do was to face Logan and say goodbye.

Resolving to leave with her dignity intact, without dropping to her knees and pleading for his love, Melissa picked up her things and left the room. As she came out the front door, Logan was talking to Rick in the courtyard. Melissa focused her attention on her videographer. "I'm ready," she said, joining them.

"I'll take your bags." Rick left to put her belongings in his truck.

Pain stabbed Melissa as she turned to Logan. "Well, I guess this is goodbye." Despite her attempt to keep her emotions under control, tears welled in her eyes.

Logan's gaze swept her as regret and sadness stole through him. A hundred men couldn't have stopped him from touching her. He stepped close, stroked her cheek with his knuckles, then cupped her neck with his hand and drew her to him. "I guess," he answered on a rough sigh. Aligning their bodies, he embraced her, then lifted her mouth to his. From somewhere deep inside him he managed a brief smile. "It's okay, sweetheart. As you said, we both knew this wasn't going to last."

Melissa choked back a sob. "I know."

"Be careful out there."

"I will." With her whispered promise between them, she raised up on her toes intent on giving him a brief kiss. But the second her lips touched his, her control shattered. She gave herself to him, body, heart and mind.

Their kiss shifted, deepened until all that remained was sensation.

Hot.

Demanding.

Touching her to her very soul.

Logan devoured Melissa's essence. He wanted to make sure she remembered what they had shared, to show her with this kiss that he loved her. Words he had no right to say. He made love to her mouth, pouring himself into the only way he could to show how much she meant to him.

And then he found the strength to let her go.

He stepped away. "Take care of yourself, sweetheart," he whispered on a harsh breath.

Aching to stay, Melissa nodded. She walked away, unable to look back. She got into Rick's truck and shut the door. As he started the engine, she caught a glimpse of Logan in the side mirror. He stood still in the courtyard, his hands on his hips, his head facing the ground.

A man alone.

A man she loved desperately.

Rick touched her shoulder and a sob escaped her lips. Melissa held her hand up to stave off any conversation. He gave her a gentle squeeze, then put the truck in gear. They traveled down the long drive, each second taking her farther away from the happiest she'd been in her life.

Memories of leaving long ago haunted her. She fisted her hands and fought off another wave of emotion as she looked out over the rolling hills and the cattle grazing in the distance.

Was she doing the right thing? Years ago she'd been a naive girl. Because she'd believed a vindictive woman, she'd doubted Logan's love. Truthfully, she'd never given him a chance.

Melissa thought about Jessamine Golden, the map and the rose petals from her purse. A woman whom legend told lived outside the law…a woman with secrets and a soft heart. A strong woman who had the courage to stand up for herself.

In every other facet of her life, Melissa faced challenges with strength and perseverance. Why not now? To leave without telling Logan she loved him would be reliving her past mistake all over again.

Logan hadn't said he loved her, but then, she hadn't confessed her love for him, either. So afraid of getting hurt by him again, she'd waited and hoped and dreamed. She hadn't given him any reason to admit his feelings for her.

She frowned. Why would he?

Ever since she'd arrived, she'd put up a front by talking about her job. Keeping a shield between them by mentioning her promotion. Though she loved her work, becoming an anchor would mean nothing without Logan in her life.

Sitting up, she wiped the dampness from her cheeks. She refused to leave without ever knowing what could have been. If there was the slightest chance that Logan loved her, it was a risk she was willing to take.

The truck cleared the cattle guard. Melissa grabbed Rick's arm. "Stop the truck!"

"What?"

They drove under the Wild Spur sign. "I said stop the truck!"

Rick slammed on the brakes and the truck skidded to a stop. A plume of dust churned past them, sweeping across the road that led to the highway a short distance away. His head whipped in her direction. "Melissa, are you all right?"

"Yes," she cried, struggling to get her breathing under control. "I've never been more all right in my life."

Rick shoved the truck into park, his expression wrought with concern. "What is it? What's wrong?"

She grabbed the handle and pushed open the door. "I can't leave." Climbing out of the truck, she looked at Rick. "Go to Houston without me. I'm going back to Logan."

Rick's eyes widened, then he grinned. "Are you sure?"

"Yes." And she was. She'd never been more sure of anything in her life.

Pride filled Rick's face. "Well, get in and I'll take you up to the house."

She shook her head and stepped back. "No, I'll walk. I need the time to gather my thoughts. Just put my stuff on the side of the road," she told him, then shut the door and started walking.

"Good luck, honey," he called as he unloaded her bags.

Melissa looked back, waved, then smiled. "I'll call you later." The engine revved behind her then faded as he drove away.

"I love you, Logan," she whispered as she continued up the driveway.

She felt a sense of homecoming. Fear of being hurt

had stopped her from admitting her feelings for the past few weeks, but she wasn't afraid anymore. Melissa had never dreamed that she would see Logan again, or that they would have a second chance. She thought she'd made peace with that. Now she knew that she hadn't really been living.

Yes, she loved working, but there was more to life than chasing stories and reporting the news. There was loving deeply—as she loved Logan. There were friends, not just coworkers. There were birthday and anniversary celebrations and holiday dinners—the kind that left you with a feeling of warmth and togetherness.

As she walked, she thought of a million things she wanted to say to Logan—all of the things she'd kept locked inside for years.

Once, a long time ago, he had asked her to marry him. That day was still vivid in her mind, one of the happiest moments in her life. She wanted to put the past behind them, give them new and special memories to share.

As she neared the house, her pulse quickened as her gaze swept first the corral, then the driveway, then finally the courtyard.

Her heart ached when she saw Logan. He hadn't moved from the spot where he'd been standing when she left.

Oh, Logan, I do love you.

Her eyes began filling with a fresh wave of tears. He must have heard her footsteps, or the whispers of her heart, because he slowly raised his head and their eyes met. Shock flashed across his handsome face. Her footsteps faltered momentarily, then she recovered and continued walking until she was only a few feet away. All the time he watched her, his eyes intense and questioning.

"What happened? Was there an accident?" Logan searched Melissa's expression as she stopped in front of him. Her eyes were red and swollen.

Melissa's auburn hair swayed as she shook her head. "No."

"What are you doing here? Did you and Rick have a fight?" What had taken place between her and Rick that she'd had to walk back to the ranch? She didn't look as if she'd been hurt, but there was a trace of wariness in her eyes.

"No, Rick is…in his truck. I came back because I needed to ask you something," she said softly.

At the raw emotion in her voice, he tensed. Did she have any idea of what she was doing to him? It had been hell letting her go. Though he'd known it was the right thing to do for her, the pain of watching her leave had crushed him. "Do you need a ride or something?" He steeled himself against doing something foolish, such as reaching out for her. If he did, this time he wouldn't be able to let her go.

A small smiled formed on her lips, warming her eyes. "No. At least I don't think so."

Confused, Logan's brows dipped. "What then?"

She stepped closer to him, and took a deep breath as she stared into his eyes. "Logan, a long time ago you asked me to marry you. At the time, I loved you so much. But I made a terrible mistake when I didn't trust you. I'm not going to make that mistake again." She released the breath on an unsteady sigh.

"Being with you these past weeks has been wonderful. No, more than wonderful. It's been amazing. Logan…I'm so in love with you that I hurt here." She placed her hand over her heart. When he started to speak, she touched her finger to his lips. "Let me finish," she said, letting her hand fall.

"Logan, will you marry me?"

Logan's breath got trapped in his lungs. "What?"

Melissa smiled. "That's not the answer I was expecting. A simple yes was what I was hoping for, unless—"

"Yes," he growled, then hauled her against him. His mouth crashed down on hers in a long, drugging kiss. Fire consumed him as their mouths mated in a heat-induced frenzy. Keeping her in his embrace, he lifted his lips and gazed into her eyes. "God, I've missed you."

She chuckled. "I've only been gone fifteen minutes."

"It's been fifteen minutes of pure hell," he confessed, holding her in his arms. "I love you, Melissa. You'd better be damned sure you love me because I'm never going to let you go. You're part of me."

"That's a relief because, for a moment, you had me worried." She wrapped her arms around his neck.

"*I* had *you* worried? When I saw you, my heart was in my throat." He stroked her hair. "I can't believe you're here. I love you so much, sweetheart. I wanted you to stay, prayed that you would."

She touched his face. "Really?"

"More than you'll ever know. I don't think I ever stopped loving you," he said. "When I saw you at the anniversary ball, I couldn't believe it. I knew then that I couldn't let you leave without touching you."

"You were so angry. When you offered us a place to stay, I didn't know what to think," she admitted.

"It was the only way I could keep you here."

"I was upset with you at the time, but that was because I didn't want you to know that I still loved you." At the time she hadn't admitted as much to herself. "I'm glad you were so persistent. I'm sorry that we lost so many years, but we have forever to make up for it." She kissed him.

"You're right." His eyes darkened.

"What matters now is we're together."

"Forever." His fingers wrapped around her neck. "It hurt so much to let you go." He had survived her leaving him years ago, but this time he'd known he would never recover.

"Why did you?" Melissa asked, gazing into his eyes. Though convinced he loved her, she needed to hear his reason.

"Watching you these past few weeks, I realized how talented you are. I know how much your career means to you. I didn't want to take that away from you."

"Logan—"

He kissed away her words, preventing her from finishing. "No, listen," he insisted, his lips hovering above hers. "We both know we can't go back all those years. You've worked hard to build your career. I told you how proud I am of you and everything you've accomplished. I meant it. Together we'll find a way to make this work."

Melissa didn't think it was possible to admire Logan more than she did at that moment. "I enjoy what I do, but it doesn't define who I am. I'm not taking the promotion."

He shook his head. "The promotion in Houston is what you've worked for. I can't let you give that up."

"I don't want to live in Houston, Logan. I want to live here on the Wild Spur, with you."

"Melissa—"

"I think Joe Fisher may have an opening at WRYL. He gave me his card and asked me to call him if I was interested in working here."

His face burst into a smile. "Really? You'd want to work here?"

Her eyes softened as she nodded. "I want to be an anchor and I can be that wherever you are. I know how much you love this ranch. I'd never ask you to give it up. I want a chance for us to enjoy each other, to discover all the wonderful things in life that we were never able to. Until now." She pressed her hand to his chest, felt the beat of his heart. "I want to take pleasure in the freedom of touching you. I want to make love whenever we feel like it. And if you're willing, I want to have your children and raise them right here."

"You want to have children?" The thought of her carrying his child made his knees weak.

"Yes, please," she whispered, loving him. "I love you, Logan. I always will."

Logan swept her up in his arms and started for the house. He'd never dreamed that when he'd seen Melissa at the Royal anniversary celebration, he'd be lucky enough to win her love again. With their past behind them, he intended to spend the rest of his life making her happy.

She laughed. "Logan, what are you doing?"

"If we're going to start on those children, then we'd better get married soon."

Melissa squealed as he carried her inside to his room. "Really?" she asked, her eyes lighting with joy.

"Sweetheart, I love you. And I've waited more than ten years to make you my wife. I'm not waiting a day longer than necessary to start a family."

Starting right now, he thought, as he began unbuttoning her blouse. "Now, what was that you said about making love whenever we feel like it?"

* * * * *

COMING NEXT MONTH

#1675 CONDITION OF MARRIAGE—Emilie Rose
Dynasties: The Ashtons
Abandoned by her lover, pregnant Mercedes Ashton turned to her good friend Jared Maxwell for help. Jared offered her a marriage of convenience…that soon flared into unexpected passion. But when the father of Mercedes's unborn child returned, would her bond with Jared be enough to keep their marriage together?

#1676 TANNER TIES—Peggy Moreland
The Tanners of Texas
Lauren Tanner was determined to get her life back on track…without the assistance of her estranged family. When she hired quiet Luke Jordan, she had no idea the scarred handyman was tied to the Tanners and prepared to use any method necessary—even seduction—to bring Lauren back into the fold.

#1677 STRICTLY CONFIDENTIAL ATTRACTION—Brenda Jackson
Texas Cattleman's Club: The Secret Diary
Although rancher Mark Hartman's relationship with his attractive secretary, Alison Lind, had always been strictly professional, it changed when he was forced to enlist her aid in caring for his infant niece. Now their business arrangement was venturing into personal—and potentially dangerous—territory….

#1678 APACHE NIGHTS—Sheri WhiteFeather
Their attraction was undeniable. But neither police detective Joyce Riggs nor skirting-the-edge-of-the-law Apache Kyle Prescott believed there could be anything more than passion between them. They decided the answer to their dilemma was a no-strings affair. That was their first mistake.

#1679 REFLECTED PLEASURES—Linda Conrad
The Gypsy Inheritance
Fashion model Merrill Davis-Ross wanted out of the spotlight and had reinvented herself as the new plain-Jane assistant of billionaire Texan Tyson Steele. But her mission to leave her past behind was challenged when Tyson dared to look beyond Merrill's facade to find the real woman underneath.

#1680 THE RICH STRANGER—Bronwyn Jameson
Princes of the Outback
When fate stranded Australian playboy Rafe Carlisle on her cattle station, usually wary Cat McConnell knew she'd never met anyone like this rich stranger. Because his wild and winning ways tempted her to say yes to night after night of passion, to a temporary marriage—and even to having his baby!

SDCNM0805